FIGHTING LOVE

He took her hand, causing her to look up, those startling blue eyes searching him—Zac, someone she barely knew—for comfort and support. Like she was a little girl so desperately in need of approval that she'd accept it from anyone. And it broke him, broke through all the doubts and chaos in his mind, all the reasons he'd given himself to stay away. Because although perhaps he wasn't inherently kind, he was a good person, and he could sense when someone needed something to keep them from falling over the edge. And Sophie Marsh didn't need just anything.

She needed him.

With one final exhale to release the last of his uncertainty, Zac edged closer to her, pulling her to him at the same time, two magnets finding their attraction. He glided his hands over her cheeks, shaking his head slowly as he took in her beautiful face. Then, with the ducks as their only witnesses, he pressed his lips to hers, his hands gently cradling her face as she rose up to him, embracing the kiss. Embracing him and his silent promise to be what she needed.

Even if eventually what she needed was for him to say good-bye . . .

Books by Melissa West

Hamilton Stables
RACING HEARTS
WILD HEARTS
SILENT HEARTS

The Littleton Brothers
FIGHTING LOVE

Published by Kensington Publishing Corporation

FIGHTING LOVE

Melissa West

LYRICAL SHINE
Kensington Publishing Corp.
www.kensingtonbooks.com

LYRICAL SHINE BOOKS are published by

Kensington Publishing Corp.
119 West 40th Street
New York, NY 10018

All Kensington titles, imprints, and distributed lines are available at special quantity discounts for bulk purchases for sales promotion, premiums, fund-raising, educational, or institutional use.

Special book excerpts or customized printings can also be created to fit specific needs. For details, write or phone the office of the Kensington Sales Manager: Kensington Publishing Corp., 119 West 40th Street, New York, NY 10018. Attn. Sales Department. Phone: 1-800-221-2647.

Lyrical Shine and Lyrical Shine logo Reg. U.S. Pat. & TM Off.

First Electronic Edition: January 2017
eISBN-13: 978-1-60183-988-6
eISBN-10: 1-60183-988-X

First Print Edition: January 2017
ISBN-13: 978-1-60183-989-3
ISBN-10: 1-60183-989-8

Printed in the United States of America

For Christi

ACKNOWLEDGMENTS

Thank you to God and my family for guiding me daily. To Jason, thank you for showing me real love so I have a frame of reference for my stories. To my daughters, you are the reason I push myself to always do and be better.

I have continued thanks to John Scognamiglio, Rebecca Cremonese, Vicki Adang, and the full team at Kensington for being such a joy to work with. Thank you so much to Nicole Resciniti for supporting this series and my work.

At this point, I could not write a book without the support of Rachel Harris and Cindi Madsen. Thank you for showing me continued friendship, keeping me sane, and reading random lines over and over again. I love you girls!

And finally, thank you to all my readers, old and new. I do this for you.

Chapter One

"**S**hit."

Zac Littleton stopped walking, balanced the two boxes he was carrying on his strong thigh, and peered over at his brother. Already he was on edge. Littleton Farms sold at the market every other Saturday during spring and summer, and yet every other Saturday, it was a damn three-ring circus to get everyone here and everything set up. So far that morning, they'd locked themselves out of a supply closet, broken two baskets, and Zac had snapped at the mayor, which was never a good idea. But Mr. Mayor refused to let them park without their vendor parking pass—somehow forgotten in the other delivery truck. "What now?"

Brady nodded his shaved blond head forward, his skin tanned from hours on the farm. Cargo shorts and a green Littleton Farms T-shirt completed his look. The market helped the farm meet its monthly goals, and without those Saturday sales, Zac wasn't sure the family farm would survive. Which wasn't an option.

The Littleton boys hadn't always run things. Zac and his brothers had used the little bit of savings they each had to open up Southern Dive, their dream dive shop, five years ago. But then their father had a massive heart attack, followed by another, and suddenly the brothers had to juggle both jobs—their dream and their obligation to the family. And for the most part, everything had been fine, business was good. The town supported them no matter what, and that loyalty was the only thing keeping the farm in the black. Despite the fact that Littleton hadn't made the expensive but ever popular switch to organic.

New age hippies pushed organic foods like it was gold and everything else was crap, and while Zac loved the idea of converting the farm, now wasn't the time. They didn't have the resources. Plus, it was easier to keep things moving than toss the lot and redo everything. And no one in town seemed to care anyway. They knew the Littletons went as natural as possible, and they respected what the farm produced. No one said a word. Well, no one except—

"Shit."

"That's what I said."

Zac's gaze fixed on the booth directly across from the Littleton Farms booth, the pink and orange and green sign for Fresh Foods Organics bright and visible for all to see. Who the hell made butterflies part of a food logo? No one, that's who.

"Ah, hell. Y'all didn't tell me we were in for a fight today." Charlie, Zac's middle brother, paused beside him and baby brother Brady, all of them staring at the vixen behind the Fresh Foods table.

Unsure what to do now and more than a little pissed that Mayor Collins hadn't warned them about this crap, Zac nodded toward their booth. "Just ignore her."

"Like that's possible," Brady said with another glare in her direction. "She's like one of those damn ladybugs that slip into your house, acting all pretty and ladybug-like, but really the thing's still a damn bug."

Charlie licked his lips and stared. "Still, she's a fine-looking ladybug if you ask me."

"No one did," Zac said, dropping the boxes he'd been carrying onto the long, rectangular table in their booth, his back to the person determined to destroy his family's image and convince years' worth of loyal customers to buy from her new, fancy, organic, non-GMO, eat-my-apple-and-you-will-fly farm. She'd already weaseled her way into Rick's Grocery, securing an organic section in the back of produce that was almost always empty when Zac went by. Not that he was checking.

"Well, well, look what the antibiotic-infused cow dragged in."

Zac shook his head and pivoted slowly to face her like he was the hero in a Marvel movie and she was the evil villain, eager to destroy the world one gluten-free muffin at a time. "Sophie."

"Zac."

"Glad you can remember my name. Now how about you use that memory of yours to pull up our agreement. You know, the one that says you'll position your booth at the other side of the market. Far, far away from mine."

Sophie's red lips curved into a Cheshire cat smile that would have earned her a role in *Alice in Wonderland*. She leaned forward, causing her blond waves to fall over her shoulders and drop down, barely brushing the table. She wore a basic white tank top with the Fresh Foods logo stretched across her perky breasts. Which Zac bet were fake, just like the rest of her.

"You know as well as I do that Mayor Collins chooses where each booth will be located."

"And you know as well as I do that he'd sell his right arm for one of your cherry yum yums."

The cat smile spread, the glint in her eyes sparkling like something out of a soap opera—right before the woman threw her glass of water or wine or whatever the hell she had in her hand on the poor, unsuspecting man who was stupid enough to talk to her.

"Now, now. That's not a very nice assumption. Why would I do a thing like that?"

Brady huffed. "Because you're a torturous wi—"

Zac threw up a hand to stop his brother from saying what the rest of them were thinking—and what would surely cause the other market vendors to choose Sophie's side over theirs. The Littletons were already in jeopardy of losing the male population every time she wore one of those flowy dresses of hers and handed out handmade, all-organic and gluten-free for Christ's sake apple pie samples.

"Let's just get set up," Zac said in an effort to rein in his brothers before one of them said something they'd regret. After all, the Littleton brothers had never had to watch what they said before. They had run the high school and taken Crestler's Key High's football team to the state title game, winning every year that one of the Littletons was on the team. And the year that all three had been in high school at the same time—Zac a senior, Charlie a junior, and Brady a freshman—they'd won every single game and shut out the Sunnyville Packers in the state championship. Add to that all three brothers being All-American in baseball, and basically, the town worshipped the brothers when they were young, and the brothers' devotion to the town only amplified that praise.

Then Zac moved away, a part of him glad to build a name for himself outside of the small town. He began his career coaching a high school team in Texas, where football might be more important than breathing good air, and married Lora. She was pregnant a year and a half later. When the nurse placed his beautiful baby girl in his arms, Zac understood real love for the first time in his life. The baby was named Carrie-Anne after his and Lora's grandmothers—his Carrie and Lora's Anne—and they were happier than he thought possible. Until they weren't. Or more specifically, she wasn't.

Lora battled depression on and off after giving birth, constantly accusing Zac of cheating. It wasn't until he discovered her with her OB-GYN that he realized her accusations were a means of freeing her own conscience. Lora left Zac and Carrie-Anne the next day, never to be seen or heard from again. From that moment on, Zac vowed to focus on no one else but his little girl. Women were evil, confusing liars who couldn't be trusted.

Exhibit A: Sophie Marsh.

"Yes, please, set up. I'd love to compare my apples to yours. Natural to pesticide-ridden, cancer-causing ones." She cocked her head, and Zac's spine stiffened, anger rising up, but he wouldn't let her get the best of him.

"What is it, Sophie? Jealous that my stock is twice as plentiful as yours?"

Her brow furrowed, the only hint that she had any expression beyond that blinding, condescending smile. "We'll see."

"Yeah, we will see. In fact . . . care to make a little wager? Hundred bucks to whoever sells the most today."

The woman beside Sophie stood then and reached for Sophie's arm to stop her, clear worry on her face. Now it was Zac's turn to smile, sure Sophie would step back and avoid getting beaten, which was sure to happen. Zac and Littleton Farms had twice as much produce to sell today and twice as many customers. She didn't stand a chance. But instead of backing away like a good girl, she stuck out her hand, poised for action.

"It's a bet."

Sophie Marsh smoothed back her long hair and adjusted her tank top, her eyes narrowing as Zac's gaze dropped to her chest and lingered there, no hint of humility in sight.

He flashed her a grin. "Just checkin' out your logo."

Her focus dropped from his green eyes and tan skin, which made her light golden skin look albino-esque, to his fitted dark gray T-shirt, a tribal tattoo peeking out from his left sleeve and climbing down his forearm, and then finally to his low-hung jeans. "Hmm, I don't see your logo." She stared pointedly at his crotch. "Must not be big enough."

Glenda choked beside her, and Sophie spun around before Zac could reply and—okay—before she revealed what she really thought of Zac and his impossibly ripped, partially tattooed, one-hundred-percent-man physique. The thought of his biceps bulging against his T-shirt sleeves as he crossed his arms flashed through her mind, and she wished she had a fan so she could temper the flush creeping up her neck.

Jerks shouldn't be allowed to be hot. There should be some universal law that Mother Nature was required to abide by. Jerks should have missing teeth and consider showers optional and think wings are a superfood. But no matter what, they shouldn't be allowed to look like Zac Littleton. Hell, or even Charlie and Brady for that matter. But the other two Littleton brothers didn't cause that traitorous flurry in her stomach the way Zac did. Something about the way he defended his family to the bone made her almost like him.

Almost.

Glenda took another sip of water, set it down, and turned around and leaned into Sophie, who took to sorting the already sorted goods behind them. "Did you just bring the enemy's *parts* into the conversation?"

Grimacing, Sophie peered over her shoulder to see a crowd already forming around the Littleton Farms table. "Somehow I don't think it hurt his ego too badly. God Almighty, why do people flock to them like that?" The crowd was three thick now, Zac laughing as he took orders and looking like her worst nightmare. And okay, hottest fantasy. But she was ignoring that little fact.

"Have you noticed the demographic?" Glenda pointed at the crowd Sophie was studying like a rare scientific discovery that she needed to uncover and identify. "They're all women, all in their twenties to forties, all staring at three men with muscles and tattoos. And then that hair."

"Right?" Sophie tossed her hands at her best friend in agreement. Glenda worked these events with her on weekends, despite Sophie begging her to join Fresh Foods full time. Of course, Glenda refused. The librarian hated to admit it, but she loved her day job too much to leave. Still, she helped at Fresh Foods every free chance she had, which was often. "I mean, what? Did their mama put expensive hair gel in her prenatals or something?"

"Something, for sure."

The two women stared at the brothers. Brady's hair was buzzed short, which must have broken the hearts of half the women in town. A month before, he'd had chin-length hair as wild as he was, never in place, and always looking like someone had just run her fingers through it. But then he cut it off. Honestly, it didn't hurt him or the rumors that surrounded him one bit.

Charlie had shaggy, brown hair with caramel streaks in it. And then there was Zac, whose hair veered more on the dark blond–light brown–don't know what color it wants to be spectrum. It stuck off his head in spikes that were less hair gel and more freshly showered and roughly styled in that I-don't-have-time-for-this kind of way.

Sophie had just narrowed her gaze to the tips of his hair to see if they were blond or brown when his gaze flicked to hers, catching her in her epic stare. His lips twitched, his whole face seconds away from laughter. He winked before returning his attention to the busty woman leaning toward him, an apple in each hand like she wanted to poison him with her ways like the witch had poisoned Snow White.

"Ugh."

"Let's focus. Maybe you should push your boobs up a little. Show off those D cups."

"You know I'm not that kind of lady," Sophie said even as she adjusted her hair and set her sights on the family making its way to her. The Littletons could take their business to all the women in this town, but Sophie would appeal to the families who wanted the best for their children. She'd be admirable about her approach . . . so long as begging still counted as admirable.

"Want to take our taste test?" Sophie asked the little boys as the family approached. "See if you can tell which is organic and which isn't. I bet you're both scientists in the making, right? Let this be your first experiment."

The boys jumped with excitement, and the mom and dad quickly followed suit, and soon the mom was coming closer. "Wow. I had no idea there was such a difference. It's . . ."

"Juicier, right?" Sophie asked. "The natural way produces smaller fruit, sure, but the fruit is better quality. It tastes better. Fresher."

"It does." The mom reached for a sample from the apple tray. "May I?"

A smile tipped Sophie's lips. "Of course. Everything is all natural, and here's a brochure that details all the research that's been conducted on GMOs and pesticides and the harmful ways they impact our next generation."

The mom glanced at her sons, and Sophie could almost hear the wheels in her brain turning, mommy mode taking over. "Hmm, I had no idea."

"Most don't, but it's time we change that. If not for ourselves, then for them." Sophie ruffled one of the boys' hair. "Don't you think?"

The woman took a bite from an apple slice and closed her eyes in satisfaction. "These are amazing."

"You should try them in my apple pie." Sophie motioned to her baked goods, and soon the family was loaded up with fresh fruit and veggies and two pies, one on the house because they'd hit the spending threshold that warranted a free dessert. And there was Sophie's angle—taste over size. Freshness over quantity.

The sweet Cartee family told their friends as they passed them, pointing toward Fresh Foods, while Sophie waved hello. She cut more pies into sample bites, more fruit into slices.

An hour passed this way before Sophie realized she was out of the crappy, nonorganic fruit so necessary to prove her point and complete the sale.

"Watch this," Sophie whispered to Glenda, who shot her that same concerned look she had given her when Sophie had said she wanted to buy the old Rochester farm and convert it to Fresh Foods. Like Sophie had drunk a gallon of trouble and was headed to the store for another.

"What are you doing?"

"Just watch."

Sophie walked around her booth, careful to smile at the crowd that now surrounded her station, to hug a little girl with pigtails who wanted to try the peach cobbler and give a brochure to a family who wanted to know the names of the things that were killing their children.

Then she strutted directly to the booth across from hers and waited patiently in line. There was still a fine crowd around the Littletons, and

Sophie couldn't for the life of her figure out why. Why would these people choose lesser quality food just because it was a little cheaper?

Her eyes fell on the basket of apples in view from where she stood, the price shining out for all to see, and she stumbled on her heels. Okay, so maybe *a lot* cheaper. Man, how did they manage those sorts of prices?

Finally, the woman in front of her finished deciding between the two pieces of fruit in her hand, one speaking to her more than the other apparently, and Sophie dropped her arms to her side and slipped on her trademark grin.

Zac was ducked down, grabbing more fruit to replenish the depleted stock, so he hadn't seen her yet, but Charlie and Brady had, and their eyes were now locked on her. Finally, Zac straightened, caught the expression on his brothers' faces, and cocked his brow before he turned to follow their glare and fix his own firmly on Sophie.

"What are you doing over here? Already throwing in the towel and offering up that hundred?"

The market was bustling now, people filing in as fast as they left, the day a perfect seventy with a light breeze in the air. Sophie loved days like this and how they reminded her of life when she was little. Long before her parents died and Nana took over raising her. Back when nothing made her happier than a blanket and sunshine and puffy clouds that made shapes. She and her daddy used to lay outside, a clothesline full of clothes around them, and stare into the sky at the magical clouds that formed and moved and told stories she'd never heard. But then everything changed.

"Actually, if you want to peek over there, you'll see we're doing pretty well. And at three times your cost per fruit. Plus, did I mention the baked goods?" She cocked her head as though she were calculating. "I think it'll be pretty hard for you to beat us."

Zac's jaw ticked. "We'll see. What do you want, Sophie?"

She produced a twenty. "I actually need to buy some fruit."

"Some fruit," he deadpanned.

"Apples and oranges please. Ten of each."

"You're joking."

She shook her head all innocent like and tried to bite back the smile threatening to take over her face. "No. I'm one hundred percent serious. I need ten of each please."

His eyes narrowed. "For what exactly?"

And here it was, the moment she would be laughing about for the rest of the day. She tried to drag it out, but Zac had placed his hands on his hips and had that alpha, you'll-tell-me-now-or-else vibe going on, and Sophie feared she'd start staring at him again instead of delivering the blow.

"See, I like to do a comparison with my samples. My organic, juicy fruit with your . . ." She picked up an apple and wrinkled her nose for effect. "Chemically derived version. Helps seal the deal with my customers."

"Do I have 'moron' tattooed on me?"

Sophie leaned in closer to Zac, careful to study the tattoo on his left forearm, then the thinner one circling his right bicep. Good God, this man needed to drop the hot card before Sophie lost her nerve. She pulled back, wishing she could take a much-needed breath, but she suspected he would see her.

"Nope. Not that I can see," she said, beaming at him. "Ten oranges, ten apples please."

The booths on either side of the Littletons' had quieted down, their eyes and gossipy ears trained on Sophie and Zac. For a moment, she considered waving to them so they'd at least pretend to ignore this, but she'd already pissed off the Littletons. The last thing she needed was to anger the rest of the town. After all, she was an outsider, moved to Crestler's Key six months ago, ready to rebuild her life. Ready to rebuild herself.

She forced herself to put the thought out of her mind before it materialized. It didn't matter now—the past was in the past.

Dropping the bill onto the change box beside the Littletons' credit card machine, she smiled at Zac and started for the basket of apples, but he reached out and grabbed her hand. His rough fingers closed around her soft ones, and before she could help herself, her eyes darted over to his and she swallowed hard.

"No."

He dropped her hand and thank God, because Sophie couldn't speak, let alone berate him. A strange, swirly feeling had blossomed in her stomach at his touch, and she wasn't sure what to say or how to say it without revealing that he had affected her. That was unexpected, and she made a mental note to not touch him again. Ever. Because she couldn't afford to show weakness around Zac Littleton, and if that tiny touch made her knees wobbly, what would full-out hugging or something do? It was too dangerous to even consider. She needed to hate him if she planned to survive this battle of the farms.

"You can't refuse to sell me fruit."

Brady and Charlie flanked Zac, and all three brothers crossed their arms like they were superheroes ready to defend the world. "Actually," Charlie said, "we can."

"That's right. Now begone, before somebody drops a house on you, too," Brady said, waving Sophie away.

Her brow furrowed. "What are you talking about?"

"You know, *Wizard of Oz*."

"I see. And you think I'm the Wicked Witch in this version of the story? Are you mad?"

"Witch, Tin Man. Same thing."

Sophie laughed despite the sting she felt. She had been the quintessential nice girl her entire life. It bothered her to know the brothers disliked her so much, the nice girl in her eager to make everyone happy. But then she was no longer that girl in more ways than one. "Ah, so either evil or heartless. Gotcha." Then she leaned in closer to the brothers. "Yet I'm not the one poisoning my customers with chemicals that should never be anywhere near food."

Several of the customers around the Littleton booth stared down at their baskets, which were a nice touch, she had to admit. Inexpensive baskets with the Littleton logo that customers could fill with fruit and then place the basket on their kitchen table or counter, the logo reminding them where to go when the contents were depleted. If she didn't despise them so, she'd have commended them on such a great idea. There was some brainstorming to be done on her end to come up with a comparable option, and she made a mental note to hit up Pinterest that night.

Brady opened his mouth to say something else, but it was Zac who spoke up.

"We can and will sell to whomever we like. Whenever we like. Now drop that apple in your hand, or I'll have Tom arrest you for stealing."

At that, Sophie laughed louder, this time a legit laugh instead of the ones she used to aggravate the brothers. "Tom." She licked her lip and urged Zac toward her with her index finger and then pointed to her booth. "That Tom?"

Zac looked like he wanted to punch the table, but Sophie had to give it to him. He held his tongue. "Leave. Now."

"No."

"Fine." Zac walked around the booth, stood over Sophie, and then in a whoosh, lifted her up, kicking and screaming, but helpless in his strong arms.

"Put me down right now!"

"Your wish is my command, madam." He dropped her into her booth and bent close. "Come into my domain again, and I'll do it again. This time on your ass. Understand?"

Flames broke across Sophie's cheeks and up her ears, her anger taking over. "You're an animal."

He smirked. "Honey, you have no idea." Then he walked back to his booth, his brothers high-fiving him and laughing, all at her expense. But this wasn't over. Far from it.

It wasn't until Sophie pulled her gaze away from Zac that she caught Prissy Tallon of *Crestler's Key Independent* to the right, her camera fixed on Sophie before snapping a picture that was sure to show up in the paper the next day.

Damn it.

Sophie flashed a smile at her customers. "You'll have to excuse us. Friendly bet going on, and poor Zac is a sore loser. Y'all should go buy something from him to make him feel a little better." She paused, her finger to lip. "On second thought, don't do that. You stay right here with me." They laughed at her, and she continued taking orders. Her eyes lifted a few minutes later, only to find Zac watching her, that condescending smirk still on his face.

One point for you, Littletons. But I'm winning this bet and this town's business whether you like it or not.

The day came to a close, the sun starting its descent behind the trees that cradled the market, and Sophie finally allowed herself to sit down and take a breath. She and Glenda had worked every second, never stopping, until there was nothing left in the booth's bakery section and only a few cantaloupes and a bag or two of lemons in produce.

A light breeze floated in the air, and Sophie thought she might just take that hundred dollars from the Littletons and do a little online shopping at that new Earth Essentials online boutique she'd stumbled across last week.

Glenda settled into the chair beside her. "Okay, I have our total for the day. Ready?" She bounced in her chair, her excitement evident.

Sophie sat up taller and stared at her friend, pride all over both of them because they knew they had this. There was no way one could work that hard for that long and not win a bet.

"Two hundred, twenty-two dollars and ninety-seven cents."

Jumping to her feet, Sophie took the slip of paper from Glenda's hands and peered at the number. It was the most they'd ever sold at the market, and it couldn't have come at a better time. "Woo-hoo!" The ladies hugged, and all was wonderful and peaceful and great in the world. Until the sound of a man clearing his throat brought them back to reality.

Sophie glanced over slowly, already sure of who'd invaded their fun. Damn fun-taker. That's what Zac Littleton's name should be. All right, so maybe that was a shade close to elementary schoolyard talk, but come on! Couldn't he let her enjoy herself for five seconds before coming over to fight again?

"What?" Sophie asked, her hands on her hips and her lips pursed because she couldn't bring herself to fake it with him right then. A grin spread across Zac's face that reminded her entirely too much of his voice, all slow and soothing in a way that made you want to do whatever you'd done again just so you could see the grin light his face again. Of course, that was if she didn't hate the pants off him. Which she did. Totally did.

And now she was thinking about him without pants on.

Gah, gah, gah.

"I asked you what you wanted."

"I was just giving you a second to collect yourself. By the way," he said, taking a step toward her, then two so he was in her space, that spicy, earthy, hint of lemony scent of his washing over her in the best and worst possible ways. "Do you ogle all men like this or just me?" He bit down on his bottom lip and stared at her with those soulful green eyes, and damn if she didn't hate him all the more.

"You think you're funny, don't you?"

"Everyone thinks I'm funny."

"Not me."

He cocked his head. "I'm not sure you count. Enemies and all. And besides, you don't really know me, now, do you?"

She opened her mouth to say that she knew him all right. She'd been with guys like him before, all beautiful face and hair and a smile that could move mountains. Until he flashed that smile at some other woman passing by, and suddenly you realized that mountain-moving sincerity wasn't just for you. It was for any skirt willing to play with him. Well, Sophie wasn't willing to play. But she knew she'd embarrass herself if she lost her cool, so instead, she closed the distance between them, glad she'd thrown on her new red heels rather than the flats she'd almost grabbed. Instead of a full head shorter than him, she was only a few inches. All right, six inches. But still, better than twelve.

Tilting her head up, she met his gaze with all the confidence of a woman who would not fail. Not today, not ever. "I have my number, I'm guessing you have yours, and that's why you're invading my personal space?"

"Hey, you're the one who closed the distance, honey. Not me."

"Stop calling me honey."

"Stop smiling all the time like you're sweet."

"I am sweet."

"So is a bee until it stings you."

Drawing a long breath, Sophie told herself to calm down and think about Earth Essentials. That maxi skirt and tank top outfit they'd released for spring would look perfect on her.

"Your number, Littleton."

"Eight five nine, four two three, two six eight seven."

Sophie thought her head might explode. "Not your phone number."

He grinned. "Thought you might need it. You know, so you could call me before you bring over my hundred bucks."

"You're not getting a hundred bucks."

"We'll see, won't we?"

Sophie counted to three in her head, like she'd heard on *Dr. Phil* that time they talked about women who lost their cool on their children. And though Sophie didn't have kids, she'd pocketed that tiny piece of advice, sure her Scorpio self could use it. And she'd been right. On more occasions than she could count.

"What? Get a little lightheaded around me?"

"Yeah, it's all that arrogance of yours. Sucks all the air from the room. Now tell me your damn number."

He was so close to laughter that Sophie contemplated challenging him to a fight instead of the bet. Maybe arm wrestling or something. Sure he was huge and she was tiny, but she needed to be aggressive with this man—manhandle him a little—before she exploded. And then, once again, her thoughts went south, and she wondered if he brought all that alpha attitude into the bedroom or if he—

Lalalala—think about something else, think about something else.

"Show me already," she said through gritted teeth.

"I'll show you mine if you show me yours." He waggled his eyebrows, and Sophie sucked in a breath, sure he'd read her mind, but then she realized that no—he'd just gotten under her skin. Again.

Needing away from this man before she did something horrible like punch him—or worse, kiss him—she held out the daily sales receipt that Glenda had given her and snatched the sheet Zac had been holding. Her eyes scanned down the printout, so much fancier than hers, until finally she reached the total. Her heart sank into her pretty heels, too embarrassed to show itself again.

"Three hundred, fifty-five dollars, twenty-two cents. How did you—" But she stopped herself before she asked what she wanted to ask. How had they beaten her by so much when she'd had her best day ever and she charged so much more for her produce? The worry worm that liked to creep around in her brain began its slimy trek, bringing with it doubt and more doubt. But she couldn't afford to show Zac how bad she felt right now, and she certainly didn't expect him to reveal how he had hit that number.

So instead, she folded up his sheet and passed it back to him, the picture of poise. "Congratulations." Then she walked over to the cash box, Glenda's expression still hopeful until Sophie shook her head and her friend fell back into her wicker chair.

"Seriously?" Then Glenda glanced around Sophie to Zac. "What do you sell—crack with apples or something?"

"Glen," Sophie warned. "It's fine. We'll get them next time." She took five twenties from the change box and walked back over to Zac, counted out the twenties into his waiting hand, then turned around as the brothers started their victory celebration.

They might have won this round, but by God, Sophie and Fresh Foods would bring down Littleton Farms if it was the last thing she did.

She just needed a plan.

Chapter Two

"Hello?" Zac called as he unlocked the front door of his cabin in the woods. He'd bought the property when he and Carrie-Anne first moved back to Crestler's Key, found a floor plan he liked, and then spent a year building the house while he worked through all the resentment and hurt he felt over Lora leaving.

It took him a long time to realize that his anger wouldn't make her come back, that it was only hurting him and his daughter. Which was the last thing she needed.

So he finished the house, put a lock on the door, and when he showed it to Carrie-Anne, he vowed to make sure she would always have what she needed, including a father who would always put her first. They hugged, tears in both their eyes, but that was the first day of putting themselves back together.

Now she was a preteen, and often it felt like she was taking care of him instead of the other way around.

"In the kitchen," she called, and the familiar pangs of guilt spiraled through his gut. But to be honest, Carrie-Anne was a caregiver by nature, and she would try to take care of him and anyone else in her life whether they liked it or not.

The smell of garlic and sauce hit Zac's nose as he moved into the kitchen and set down a spare box of fruit and veggies and a Bundt cake he'd bought from AJ&P Bakery's booth. "Got your favorite."

Carrie-Anne stopped stirring whatever Italian dish she was making and came over to hug her dad. "Ugh, you smell horrible." She wrinkled her nose and waved her hand through the air, causing Zac to laugh.

"I've been at the market all day."

The twelve-year-old faked a cough and fanned her nose again. "How did you sell anything smelling like that?"

"Well . . . I might have gone by the farm after."

"And there's my daddy. How is the strawberry patch looking this year? Mrs. Campbell asked me about it after class today. She wants to do a field trip there in a few weeks."

"It's good. I think we'll be fine for the first U-Pick this weekend."

Carrie-Anne's face lit. She always loved when the kids came out to the farm, loved helping them find the biggest strawberries in the patch. And he loved watching her feel so happy. It made him think she'd put her mother leaving behind her, even if Zac still hadn't.

"Great! I'll tell Mrs. Campbell. And I can send an e-vite again this year if you want? Maybe put something on the school's Facebook page?"

"I don't want you to worry over it. I can have someone post on our page to get the word around, and then this is Crestler's Key. Word will spread."

"I know." She stirred the sauce again. "But I like helping. You shouldn't have to do it all by yourself."

Zac felt the familiar knot in his throat rising. "Now, you know better than to worry about me, Carrie-Bee. I'm just fine."

She shrugged, glanced over her shoulder at him, then back at the pot.

"Okay, I know that look. Is there something else on your mind?" Zac asked as he grabbed some plates from the cabinet and set the table, then poured them each a glass of sweet tea.

"It's just . . ." She trailed off, and Zac feared something horrible was coming. Something like when she got her first period, and they both thought she had internal bleeding until he called his sister, Kate, and she came over and explained that he was an idiot. Which truthfully, he should have known by now.

"What is it?"

"I was just wondering . . . you know. Well . . . why don't you date, Daddy? Reagan Prictor's parents got divorced, and her mama's already dating that new plumber that joined Drain It. Seems to really like him, and Reagan asked me if you ever date, and I said no, which she thought was odd. Is it odd? I don't know. Because I think you probably should. So why don't you? Date, that is." She turned to face him, her long brown hair hitting at the middle of her back, her skin the same olive tone as her mother's. If not for those green eyes staring at him, the very same as his, she'd look nothing like him.

"I date."

"Not that I've ever seen."

"Well, I'm not going to bring women around here, Carrie-Anne. That's not right."

She paused while scooping pasta onto their plates. "It's not wrong."

"I don't need anybody else messing with our lives."

"But maybe she won't mess with our lives." Her gaze hit his, and he realized in that moment that maybe this wasn't just about her wanting him to have a lady around the house. Maybe she wanted one, too.

"Sweetie, I . . ." But what could he say?

"I'm not saying you need to go marry Sophie Marsh or anything."

He choked on a sip of sweet tea and coughed out a laugh. "Yeah, wouldn't hang your hat on that one."

"She is pretty, though."

"Yeah. Pretty evil."

"Dad!" Carrie-Anne giggled, and he pulled her to him for another hug.

"Look, I'm sorry. I thought I was protecting you by keeping it just us, but I never thought that maybe you needed something more than me."

She shook her head. "Oh, no, Daddy, I'm not saying that. You're great. I just . . ."

"I know. And it's okay. How about I agree to try?"

A tiny smile found its way across her face. "You'll date?"

"I already date occasionally. But I'll do it a little more now. How's that?"

"Perfect. And while we're talking about dating . . ." She scooped a bite of noodles onto her fork, but didn't take a bite. "Well, Reagan and I were talking, and her mama's mentioned you a few times, so we thought maybe—"

"No. No way in he—" He caught himself as Carrie-Anne raised her eyebrows. "Heck. I was going to say heck."

"Sure you were."

He laughed again, then they dove into their fettuccini Alfredo, hunger taking over. "Mmmm, this is amazing. Grandma teach you how to cook this?"

She beamed. "Aunt Kate."

He nodded as he swirled some noodles around his fork and took another large bite. "I'll have to thank her next time I see her. You can cook, kid. I'll give you that."

"While you're thanking her, you could ask if she has any single friends."

"I said I'd try."

"No reason not to start trying now."

Zac scratched his chin and then ran his hand through his hair. "You're not going to give up on this, are you?"

"Just a few dates, Daddy."

"Right."

The problem was, Zac wasn't sure he could open his heart enough to truly date anyone. The only person he'd even considered was Becca Stark, and she'd been head over heels for Nick Hamilton. Still, what he needed was someone like her—good and wholesome without a ton of baggage and without a wealth of expectations. But how fair was that? He had baggage for days, and what was wrong with a lady expecting a thing or two? Nothing.

Only Zac wasn't so sure he could meet any of those expectations . . . and then what?

But as he watched his daughter watching him, he knew he'd have to give it a try. If not for himself, then for her.

Sophie sat outside on her wrap-around porch in a rocking chair with two broken slats that she couldn't bring herself to throw out. Her grandmother used to rock in it every evening, a cup of tea in her hand, her gaze on the stars popping on in the night sky.

Sophie used to ask her what she was thinking about, and Nana would always answer, "Before." They'd sit in silence then, Nana's mind on her time as an Army nurse and a thousand experiences that no one should have had, and no one would ever know. Never once did Nana reveal any of the horrors she'd witnessed. If not for those evenings on the porch, Nana's face strained from the effort to appear indifferent, nothing but sadness in her eyes, Sophie might have thought it hadn't affected her.

Now, as an adult, Sophie knew the hard truth—everything affects a person. A laugh at the wrong moment that reads as an insult. Sending a call to voicemail. Ignoring someone you know in the grocery store because you're too busy to say hello. Minor moments remain ingrained in our subconscious forever. Something like war? Well, it was no wonder PTSD existed and far too many sought out the relief of a bottle.

Rocking back again, Sophie ran her foot lightly over her gray tabby cat, Petite, who'd taken to being petted in this way while Sophie worked on her laptop, and now stubbornlyt refused to be petted in any other way. Taking another sip of her green tea, because apparently Nana had affected her too somewhere along the way, Sophie tried to make sense of her thoughts.

Her pesky thoughts weren't focused on something as significant as war; though if she were honest, she felt like she'd entered one in Crestler's Key without realizing it. Now she couldn't seem to find a way out of the fight, and the ridiculousness of it was that she kind of enjoyed it. She enjoyed those little laughing smiles of Zac's and the way he supported his family to a fault. Even the way he coddled his daughter on purpose so she'd roll her eyes and push him away.

It was a super hard thing to hate someone and also like him. The conflicting emotions made Sophie's head ache, and she tried to think of some new reasons to hate Zac Littleton. Like maybe he refused to let women get certified at that dive shop of his. But she knew a few ladies around town who'd gone through the training, likely just to see the brothers in a wet suit. And now, all Sophie could see was Zac in a wet suit. Then her thoughts drifted to him without that wet suit on, and Sophie's cheeks lit despite the fact that no one was around.

Sophie shook her head to try to regain some semblance of respectable thought. "The tea's jacked up my brain again, Petite," she said to the cat. Immediately she cringed because she'd become that lady—the one whose closest friend was her long-haired cat. That thought made Sophie want to throw on her best dress and heels and go into town. But then, this was Crestler's Key, and most everything was closed. She could head to that bar in Triple Run, but it seemed like everyone who went there ended up marrying a man from Triple Run and never moved back home. Which sounded nice, except Sophie owned Fresh Foods; it was her dream and passion, and she refused to let a man interfere with her dream. So there would be no going to Triple Run's bar and no risking meeting a man who could take over her world.

She had already had a man like that, and she planned never to go there again. Plus, day by day, it felt like a man was already attempting to control her life—or at least her business.

Sophie thought of Zac Littleton carrying the boxes of fruit and vegetables, his arm muscles tight from the effort, his face as relaxed as ever, and those worn jeans and how perfectly they clung to his—

"Nope, nope, nope."

Pushing out of her rocker, she stormed inside and decided that, a hundred dollars or not, what she needed was a little shopping therapy at Earth Essentials. Shopping always made her feel better . . . for a moment. Until that newness wore off and she was left with all the same thoughts zipping around in her brain. Thoughts no longer silenced by instant gratification.

But what she *really* needed to do was talk to someone who knew Zac so she could get insider details. Like how the heck he sold over a hundred dollars more than her. Seriously, how was that even possible? Did the whole Little League team buy a dozen of everything? Or maybe the choir at the giant Baptist church? Those ladies liked to power walk like it was their job, which tended to equal fruit and smoothies and energy stuff, right? So maybe them. Or maybe . . .

Sophie chewed her thumbnail and thought about it. Then thought about it some more. Finally, she couldn't simply *think* about it anymore. She needed to do something.

Grabbing the phone book that was still delivered to her door every three months, despite the fact that nobody needed a phone book anymore or even looked at one, she flipped through the names until she found the one she was looking for. She dialed the number before she could chicken out.

The phone rang three, then four times, and it was then that Sophie realized the time and that maybe they were both sleeping and she was going to ruin the little girl's day tomorrow and maybe she had a test and now she would fail and it would all be Sophie's—

"Hello?"

"Oh my God."

"Well, actually, most people call me Zac. Or 'Hey, dude.' But sure, you can go with God."

"I wasn't calling you God."

"But you *were* calling me."

Sophie stomped her foot and cursed to herself, except she must not have kept it to herself, because the next thing she knew, Zac was laughing. Loudly. A full-body kind of laugh, the kind that rumbled from deep within a person.

"What?"

"You call me, and then you get mad because I called you out on calling me? What sense does that make? Ah, right. About as much sense as you thinking you were going to win that bet today."

"I can't stand you."

"Man, not many people admit to hating God, but whatever works for you, honey."

"I didn't call you God."

"Sure you didn't."

"Oh my God!"

"See."

"I'm hanging up now."

"All right, but you won't have any resolution to whatever made you call if you hang up."

Sophie's temper boiled over, her fingers and toes and stomach all tensed for a fight. She'd never met a man who behaved as arrogantly as Zac, and suddenly she regretted every positive thought she'd ever had about him.

"I called to ask how you cheated."

"Wait, wait, wait." He chuckled softly, the sound so delicious she almost sighed—before yelling at herself to pull it together. Once again, she wished Zac had some horrible habit that would make her less attracted to him. Maybe he smoked. No, no way did he smoke. Not with super white teeth like his. She'd have to find something to secure this hate before it turned into something really dangerous.

Like a crush.

"Did you just call me a cheater?"

"I didn't call you a cheater. I asked *how* you cheated. Not the same thing."

"It's exactly the same thing. So let me get this straight. You're so arrogant that you can't possibly think you could lose fair and square. It *has* to be the other person is cheating."

"I'm arrogant?"

"I know. That's what I said."

Sophie was pacing her house now, her bare feet slapping against the hardwood floors with the weight of her rage. "That wasn't a statement, it was a question. Gah, where did you go to school?"

"Wow. And now you're questioning the educational system here in Crestler's Key? Hmm, I bet the *Independent* would be interested to hear about that. Care to give an official statement?"

"Don't you dare."

His laugh filled the void again. "I'm just messing with you. I wouldn't wish the *Independent* on my greatest enemy."

"Which is me."

"Obviously."

For some reason, that bothered Sophie more than it should have, but she pushed it away. "Back to the topic. I want to know how you outsold me by so much today."

"I'm sure you do, but magicians never reveal their tricks."

"So it wasn't real? You faked it. I knew it couldn't be real," she said, almost more to herself, and for the first time that night, she felt a bit of relief.

"Now, now. Don't get carried away with yourself. That's not what I said. How about this—you tell me how much it cost you to convert Freddie's farm to organic, and I'll tell you how I kicked your ass today."

"You didn't kick my ass."

"So a hundred bucks more than you doesn't qualify as a good ass kicking? Tell me, then—what does count as an ass kicking? Two hundred? Five? I need to be able to adequately prepare."

"Hold up. You've sold five hundred dollars at the market before?"

She could almost hear his smile and immediately resented her inability to keep her mouth shut and her opinions to herself. It was one of the reasons she'd failed so miserably at nearly every job she'd ever had. There was professionalism, and then there was watching people get treated poorly day in and day out, all while not saying a word.

It wasn't lost on Sophie that she, a mere executive assistant, had defended the staff to her old boss, but at the time she couldn't defend herself to the person closest to her.

Shaking her head, she pushed the thought away. She was finally doing what she loved, but every month her stress level climbed higher and higher. Production costs on the farm were insane, and she couldn't afford the equipment she needed to speed things up. So she was stuck producing only what she could produce, praying come spring she would reap the benefits of her hard work. And she had . . . a little. But Fresh Foods was still a long, long way from being a lucrative farm.

Turning her frustration back on the problem at hand, or in this case, at phone, she said, "I'm listening. What, did you convince the hospital to buy apples for all the patients or something?"

She heard the sound of a screen door opening and then flapping shut, then Zac adjusting the phone. "What are you doing?"

"I'm sitting on my front porch if it's okay by you."

"Doing what exactly?"

"What the hell is this? Twenty questions?"

Sophie cleared her throat. "I just want to know how you outsold me."

"The truth?"

"Always."

"Is that number you showed me your norm?"

Sophie poured another cup of hot water and dropped a teabag of English Breakfast in it, needing something more than the green tea she usually drank in the evenings. She contemplated whether she should tell him the truth—that it had been her best day—or lie and say she did that all the time. But the problem with lies, even a tiny white one like this, was that they always seemed to track Sophie down at the worst possible times and expose her. She learned at age twelve—when she'd found the rainbow butterfly eraser in the hall after school, only to learn Missy Bench had lost hers and was asking everyone if they'd seen it—that she was as bad at lying as she was at sports. And don't even get her started on sports.

"Is it?" Zac pressed. She could hear the soft sway of something in the background on his end. If he was in a rocking chair, she was going to lose it. Which was stupid. Everyone rocked in the South. It was the great Southern pastime.

Frustrated yet again with her inability to keep her mouth shut, she bit her lip, only to give in to her curiosity a half second later. "What is that sound? Are you in a rocker?"

"Good God, woman. Want to know what I'm wearing, too?"

"Funny." But now that very question was circling around in Sophie's head, and she had to bite her lip hard to keep from asking it. She needed to go see a doctor, someone to rid her mind of this disease called lust that had polluted it. Because that was what it had to be. Lust. Nothing more. And who could blame her when the guy on the other end of the phone looked like Zac?

"I thought so."

"Thought so what?"

"That it was funny."

"It was a high."

"Picturing me naked?"

Sophie choked on her tea, and Zac's rumbling laughter hit her ears. "Sorry, that was wrong. You just make it so easy."

"Trust me, I'm picturing you in a lot of different ways right now, and none of them is as satisfying as nudity."

"So seeing me naked would bring you satisfaction?"

"Ugh! Just tell me how you did it?"

She heard the whining sound stop. "I'm in a porch swing. Made it for Carrie-Anne, but honestly, it's become more my space than hers. And if that's your high, then you need to revamp your business. Not trying to tell you how to do things, but damn."

"Sounds like you're doing just that."

"Look, we don't like each other. I get that. I'm a thorn in your side."

"Understatement of the year."

"All I'm saying is maybe you want to explore other markets in the area, too. Go to Lexington. Maybe that big one in Chattanooga. Whatever. But find other ways to make money. It's hard, farming. And you need to think outside the box to keep your numbers steady. That's why we started U-Pick and put in all those kid activities. Brings the whole family out, and they feel like the money is worth it."

"Why are you telling me all of this? If I didn't know any better, I'd say you were offering me help."

Zac went silent, the pause growing long, nothing to fill the void but the grasshopper-and-frog melody that kept Sophie company each evening.

"Honestly? I don't know. Personality flaw."

"What, being a know-it-all?"

"Helping people."

They were quiet again, and Sophie thought maybe there was more to Zac Littleton than met the eye. Or maybe he'd had a few too many beers and drunk Zac was nicer than sober Zac. She couldn't be sure.

"Thanks. I'll think about it."

"You do that."

"And we're back to the arrogance."

That warm chuckle of his hit her again, and despite everything, Sophie found herself closing her eyes, basking in the sound for a moment.

"Make that two personality flaws."

She grinned. "Good night, Zac."

"Sleep tight. Try not to picture me naked." Then he hung up, and Sophie laughed to herself. Now there was nothing else she could think about.

Well played, Littleton. He'd won. Yet again.

Chapter Three

"So what'd you do with that hundred?" Charlie asked as he slid a knife blade over the tape that sealed a box of inventory.

It was Monday, which meant Zac had to jump from Southern Dive to the farm in hopes of staying ahead, only to end the day exhausted and with a to-do list a mile long for Tuesday. It was impossible to complete everything on a Monday.

"What hundred?" Zac asked as he ripped open his box by brute strength and then grinned at his brother.

"Show-off."

"Hey, it's not my fault you're a weak ass."

"Now, now, boys," Brady said as he walked out from the fitting room dressed in a new wet suit that had just been delivered from a new supplier.

"Think I'll keep this one."

Charlie rolled his eyes and started putting out the new Littleton Farms T-shirts from his box. "You keep something new every other week."

"Do not."

"Do too."

The fight continued until Zac felt his head slicing in two and said, "Enough," interrupting the fight just as he had a thousand times when the boys were younger, which wasn't lost on them.

"Who died and made you boss?"

Zac stared at Brady, who tossed up his hands in surrender. "All right, fine. New topic, and this is an important one. Can I or can I not ask out Sophie Marsh?"

Zac dropped the water bottle he'd been holding, the Southern

Dive red-and-black logo facedown on the floor, and glared at his brother. "Hell no you can't ask her out. What the hell is wrong with you?"

He expected Charlie to back him up, but when he peered over at him as if to say, *can you believe this dumb ass,* he instead found Charlie staring at him like he'd just witnessed something profound.

"What?"

Brady answered. "You like her."

"I like her more than I like you right now." Zac scowled and went back to work tearing open more boxes, though he still hadn't emptied the first box. He didn't care. He needed to work off some of this aggravation, though to be honest, he didn't fully understand why he felt so aggravated.

It all started last night after he and Sophie had gotten off the phone, her voice still clear in his mind. Then the damnedest thing imaginable happened—he was disappointed. Disappointed they'd ended the call, disappointed he couldn't continue sparring with her, disappointed he couldn't hear her voice go all sonic when he got under her skin. Which was this side of crazy. He hated Sophie Marsh. Her very presence was like a splinter in your finger that even the finest needle couldn't dig out. Annoying. Judgmental.

And hot as hell.

He jerked back at the thought, turning over the box of water bottles, which earned him a fresh round of questioning looks from his brothers.

"What now?"

"God, you do like her." Charlie this time, which worried Zac because Charlie was like a Littleton problem whisperer. Whether one of their parents, Kate, Brady, or Zac was having a problem, Charlie could always sniff it out, and then he'd listen until it was resolved. He'd missed his calling, if you asked Zac, because the man should have been a shrink. But then he was always family first, everything else second, just like the rest of them. Which may have been why he didn't blink when Zac and Brady mentioned opening Southern Dive.

"I don't like her. I like ingrown hairs more than I care for this woman. So y'all can both close your mouths." Then he shot a glare in Brady's direction. "But that doesn't mean you can ask her out, either. She's the enemy."

"True enough, and she seemed pretty busy, too. I'm surprised we won the bet."

In truth, so was Zac. People had surrounded the Fresh Foods table the entire day, pies and turnovers and fruit baskets being snapped up like candy. And for half a second, Zac had been worried, but then his trusty regulars came by—the high school football team, church group after church group—all stocking up for events that week, and before long, they had nothing left to sell except some okra and a few bruised apples.

He'd wanted to ask Sophie what she charged for her stuff, how she positioned it—single piece or a bundle—to get a better feel for how her best day would have been Littleton Farms' worst, but he couldn't bring himself to ask. If he had, she'd have pushed him on how he'd sold so much, when in truth he really hadn't sold that much. He just didn't have as much produce to sell as usual.

Which was another concern altogether.

"I think she's got her stuff overpriced. Talked to her last night, and she said that was a good day for her. Sounded like her best."

Brady smirked at him and propped a box against his hip, still wearing the new wet suit because the fool insisted on "testing" everything they received . . . and keeping half of it for himself. "Wait a sec. Did you just say last night? What, did you use the hundred to buy sexual favors or something?"

"You're a moron," Charlie said before Zac could even open his mouth.

"Hey, a man can dream." Brady dropped the box he'd been holding, opened it, and pulled out new masks. Immediately, he slipped one onto his face. "Check this shit out. Fancy."

"Not to support the moron's claims, but what were you doing talking to Sophie last night?"

Zac finished setting up the water bottles and went to work on the magnets. "Hell if I know. *She* called *me*. Wanted to talk about how we beat her by so much, but then she ended up even more disappointed after I told her that was a low for us."

Charlie kept working on the T-shirts, this time the Southern Dive shirts, his head down, but Zac could tell he was thinking. "How long did y'all talk?"

"I don't know. I didn't time the damn thing."

Brady whistled. "Sure are defensive."

"Shut it."

He grinned, and Zac contemplated asking his mother for birth records to show that he was in fact a blood brother and not adopted.

"Hey, just calling it like I see it."

"Look, she called me. We talked. About business. It wasn't a big deal."

"Are you going to talk again today?"

"No."

"And if she calls you?"

"Then she does. Dude, y'all sound like the women down at the salon. This was two businesspeople discussing their businesses." And him being naked, but he wasn't about to mention that. Or why he'd had so much fun screwing with her.

"All right, all right. But maybe it's not a bad idea."

Zac glanced up at Charlie, now across the store, tucking the shirts into their rightful slots on the back shelf. "What's not a bad idea?"

He shrugged. "You know, you talking to a woman."

Zac stared a hole into Charlie's back until he turned around. "Is there something y'all want to say?"

"Not with that attitude," Brady said. "But I'll go there anyway. Dude, you need to get laid. Badly. I tried to get Charlie to let me hire you a lady, but he thought that'd just piss you off."

Damn. First Carrie-Anne, now his brothers? Did all of Crestler's Key think he needed to date? He'd flirted with a few women in town, went out occasionally, but yeah, if he were honest with himself, it'd been a while since he'd had sex. Certainly with anyone that mattered. The few times he'd had sex after dating a woman for a little while, he was left feeling empty inside, lost on what he was doing. Zac had never been the kind of guy to sleep around. He wasn't Brady, even if there were times he wished he were.

And it wasn't like he didn't have opportunities. He had them. All the time. Women liked to try for nonchalant—at the grocery store, eating out, when they picked up orders at the farm. And he enjoyed the attention as long as he didn't have to take it further than flirting. That always ended badly for Zac—him the asshole who refused to commit, her angry that he hadn't said so from the beginning. Even though he had. Numerous times.

"Don't get pissed off, man," Charlie said. "We're just saying it wouldn't be a bad idea to go out with someone. Have a little fun."

"I have fun."

"Since when? You're boring as hell."

And just like that, his patience with the littlest Littleton had reached its max. He grabbed one of the stress balls from the counter and, when Brady turned, chucked it at him, forever a pitcher. It smacked Brady square in the back of the head.

Charlie broke into fits, and Zac smiled. "You were saying?"

Brady rubbed his head where the ball had connected. "How the hell do you hit a man from behind? What kind of wussy shit is that?"

Zac tossed his hands out. "Want to throw? I'm standing right here. Take a hit."

Brady scowled. "Like that'd go over well. You two would just team up on me like when we were kids. Plus, you're a giant or something. Still haven't figured out how you managed to get so much bigger than me. Sign with the devil or something?"

"It's called the gym. Might try it."

"Yeah, no. I do other things for cardio. *You* might try it." Brady waggled his eyebrows. "And in case my point is lost on you, I'm talking about sex."

The brothers all laughed, relaxing into their roles.

"You know, I've heard of it."

"Like this year? 'Cause these things change. Women want freakier things now. They're all reading that erotica shit and asking you to spank them and looking around for your red room." Brady shuddered. "My ass is still bruised from last weekend."

Their laughter boomed through the room then, all of them unable to rein it in. Zac thought that despite his romantic life, he was happy. Very happy. He had a great family and an even greater kid. What else could a man ask for?

Sure, he might be lonely at night when Carrie-Anne was in bed and the house became too quiet and there was nothing but crap on TV and it was raining outside, nothing to occupy his thoughts but thoughts, most of them as condemning as a judge. What did he do? Why did she leave? Wasn't he enough?

Zac sighed. Maybe they were right—maybe he did need to date. But how did one go about that in a town where everyone talked about everything? Asking Becca out had been easy—she lived in Triple Run, and he never thought that would go anywhere. But this was different. People were paying attention and expecting him to be more active.

Zac just had to figure out who to ask out without the whole town going ape-shit and planning their wedding. Which might be the hardest thing of all.

Hmm, who did Zac know who could keep this to herself, but still knew the other ladies and could make recommendations? Not Kate. She'd tell his parents and then all the Hamiltons, and he could barely stand them. Not Donna at the salon, though she tried to not gossip.

Then it occurred to him—Sophie. Sophie knew the town but wasn't really a part of it yet. She hung out in all those town meetings, had her hair and nails done at the salon, and ate at all the restaurants, all in an effort to immerse herself in the town so she could get more business. But how could Zac ask Sophie for dating advice? He couldn't, wouldn't. No way in hell.

Still . . . what if he did?

Sophie parked her Mini Cooper outside Donna's Hair & Nails, her eyes trained on the slew of women inside. She'd studied the salon for months now, careful to pay attention to when specific women arrived for their regular appointments. Which was probably über-stalkerish of her, but a woman had to do what she had to do.

Today, the salon bustled with the minister's wife, the elementary school assistant principal, and Annie-Jean Carlisle, half of AJ&P Bakery. These three women could secure contracts that would feed Sophie's starving budget for a year . . . if only they'd agree to purchase from her instead of her competition.

She thought of her call with Zac again, that smirk of his so evident in his voice that she wished she had been at his house so she could waggle her finger at him and tell him to turn that smirk on someone else. She wasn't shopping.

But then he'd said that bit about being naked. *Twice*. And suddenly Sophie's aggravation at arrogant Zac had been replaced with aggravation at herself and her dusty libido.

In truth, she hadn't intended to avoid men. It was just that when you were burned as badly as Sophie had been burned and turned your life upside down to start over, you tended to tread lightly and then take three steps back before attempting it all over again.

Fear was a debilitating thing, and Sophie felt fear down to her toes every time she thought about venturing into the dating world again. Because the problem with dating was that the bad stuff, the really bad stuff, didn't show until you were already too invested to walk away.

That fear Sophie so hated worked through her again, but she refused to let it take hold. Not anymore.

Instead, she packed her fridge magnets and pretty pens in her giant Fresh Foods tote and stepped out of her Mini Cooper. She needed an SUV for all of her hauling, but she'd never once met an SUV that looked or felt like her. She liked sweet, cute things. Pretty and simple. Just like her Mini Cooper. Maybe whoever made the Mini Cooper needed to create an SUV and then she'd relent and buy one. She'd write a letter to them tonight.

But right now, she had bigger fish that needed frying.

Sophie became a cat on the prowl, her target in sight, and already she imagined the women agreeing to support her. Female power and all that stuff, and maybe she'd push that very idea: Support me, a Southern woman just like you, brought down by a man. The feminism angle could help, so long as the women supported women's rights. Which they were sure to, right? They were women.

White clouds floated in the forever-blue sky, not a bit of humidity in the air, the sun not burning up everything yet. Pollen aside, spring had always been her favorite season. It made her happy and hopeful—flowers bursting with fresh blooms, birds singing, the scent of freshly mown grass in the air. Which made it the perfect time for her to push her organic produce on anyone with an open hand and an empty belly.

With another deep breath for courage, Sophie pulled open the salon's door, a soft jingle hitting her ears while the earthy yet slightly spicy scent of Aveda products filled her nose. Donna had switched to Aveda three months before, and Sophie had sped over, planning to talk natural products and suggest they have tea sometime to talk about the environment. Sophie thought she might also talk Donna into giving out Fresh Foods magnets and other goodies to her clients. But instead of any of that happening, Sophie had sped over, only for the salon owner to stare at her from behind those blunt black bangs of hers, her hair forever cut in a perfectly shiny bob, and turn away, the words, "I'm a Littleton Farms girl," floating out from behind her.

And that was that.

Later she learned Donna and Kate Littleton were good friends in high school, so it stood to reason she'd follow her friend. But what Sophie didn't understand was how Kate could leave Crestler's Key for a Triple Run guy, most traitorous of all traitorous moves, yet they still supported her over Sophie.

Still, that was three months ago, and Sophie had made a lot of headway since then in gaining friendships in the town. Or at least they tolerated her.

And to prove that very point to herself, she walked up to the main counter and beamed at the girl standing behind it, twenty at best, her gaze focused on her black nails like they held the answers to the universe. Or perhaps more importantly, her next date.

"Hey there," Sophie said.

The girl glanced up, her highlighted hair pulled back into a ponytail, her dark roots as obvious as a coffee stain on a white shirt, which had to be driving Donna crazy.

"You're uh . . ." Crap. What was her name?

"Zoey. Same as I told you last time you were here."

Double crap. "Right. I knew that." Sophie flashed a smile that was met with complete disdain. "I have an appointment. Ten thirty?"

"I know, Ms. Marsh. I booked it for you. You know, when you called last week, and I answered, 'Donna's, this is Zoey'?"

Triple crap. "Of course."

"You can have a seat. Trish will be with you in a second. Want some water or something?"

"Sure, that would be great."

"Lime or lemon in it?"

"Lemon, thank you." And suddenly the wheels in Sophie's brain began to spin because she'd forgotten that Donna put fresh fruit in her teas and waters. Peach or lemon in the teas, lemon or lime in the water. This was perfect! She could offer to stock them for Donna at a discount, even hand deliver them, in exchange for Donna handing out pens and magnets. Or, wait. Wait, wait, wait! Maybe she could ask to have a tea party at the salon. Yes! Delicious pastries and fresh fruit, coupled with organic teas. It would be perfect.

Now, she just had to figure out how to ask Donna without getting another glare in response.

Zoey returned with the water, and Sophie sat down and began looking through the hairstyle books to find something new to try, though she knew she'd smile at Trish and ask for a trim, then call it a day. With her trims and manicures and eyebrow waxes, she found herself at Donna's every other week it seemed like. Surely that level of business earned her a chance to talk to Donna about carrying Fresh Foods, right?

Well, today, she would find out.

Her gaze cut over to the windows beside her, a smile forming, until she locked on a truck parking outside AJ&P Bakery. Zac stepped out, dressed in rugged jeans and a green Littleton Farms T-shirt, work boots on his feet, an Atlanta Braves cap on his head. Her excitement melted away. She watched as he turned around, her eyes dropping to his backside before she could tell herself to be good, and damn. The man could fill out a pair of jeans better than any man she'd ever seen. Forcing herself to look away from Zac's impressive assets—seriously, this was becoming a problem—she watched him go around to the back of his truck and pull out a Littleton Farms crate full of apples.

Patty, the P in AJ&P, opened the door, and he kissed her cheek as he swept inside, then came back out for another crate of apples, then one with a variety of berries—strawberries, blackberries, blueberries. Everything needed for the delicious cobblers and pies sold at the bakery. When he was done, he grabbed a bouquet of flowers from the passenger seat and handed them to Patty, the sixty-eight-year-old beaming like he'd just asked her on a date. Good God, he was good.

But two could play that game.

Sophie could bring them flowers and kiss their cheeks. Annie-Jean, the AJ in AJ&P, was in this very salon. She'd kiss her cheek right this second!

Okay, maybe not this second, but she'd work that in somehow.

"Sophie? You ready?"

She glanced up to find Donna a few feet away.

"Um, yes. Is Trish not here today?"

"She had to leave all of a sudden. Morning sickness."

"Oh, wow. I didn't even know she was pregnant."

Donna waved her on. "I know it. Girl's a pencil, and she's three months in. By then, I already looked like a balloon ready to pop."

With a soft laugh because you could never tell if a woman wanted to be laughed at about things like weight or simply reassured that it wasn't true, she followed the shop owner to the back of the black, white, and pink salon to the very last station—Donna's station. The chair so few women in town were privileged enough to sit in because Donna stayed booked. Sophie couldn't believe her luck! Finally, she'd have Donna's ear for a solid amount of time. Now she just had to figure out a way to lengthen it.

"Just a trim?"

"Um, actually . . ." Sophie drew a breath, sure she'd lost her mind, but she needed to do this if she wanted to be in Donna's good graces. "I was thinking of adding some layers. And highlights? Really, whatever you think. I want to try something new."

Something new? Dear God, what was she thinking? Visions of her long hair chopped off in one of those boy cuts all the celebrities wore flashed through her head, and she released a whimper before she could silence it.

"Or just something simple. What-whatever you think?"

Donna's lips curved into a grin, and she clapped her hands together excitedly. "I have been itching to get a hold of this long mane. Are you sure anything goes?"

Forcing back the urge to cringe and run from the salon, Sophie nodded. "Um, sure. I just need to keep a lot of the length so I can pull it back in a ponytail. Gotta keep it back when I'm baking and stuff."

Donna nodded as she walked around Sophie, lifting her hair and dropping it, then cocking her head in thought. "What do you think about red? I think you'd look amazing as a strawberry blond."

"No!" Then she cleared her throat. "Um, what I meant to say was, no, I've never considered it. But I think that could be real nice." She needed some vodka. Stat.

"How about we take it slow? We'll add layers and then blond and strawberry highlights. It'll look fantastic."

"Sounds perfect," Sophie said, her smile tight. What was strawberry hair color? Like pink red? Oh God. She forced herself to draw a breath and calm down. It was just hair, it'd grow out, and she could dye it back if she hated it. But then she realized that no, she couldn't, because she'd offend Donna and in turn lose any good favor she gained from the experiment. She would be stuck like this, like it or not.

Deep breath. Deep, long breath.

Donna went to the back to mix the various hair dyes and then returned with a tray of little bowls and several sheets of aluminum foil.

"Um, what's that?"

A laugh came from the stylist beside them. "Gah, honey, haven't you ever had highlights before?"

Sophie bristled, but tried to keep her cool. She wanted to tell her, no, she'd grown up poorer than dirt. Nana did everything she could just to keep food on the table, so Sophie wasn't about to waste hundreds of dollars on silly things like hair color when she'd have the rest of her life to worry about that. Like when gray set in, because although Sophie hadn't colored her hair yet, she knew that day was coming. Like it or not. Nana was full on white-haired now, so Sophie thought she might follow in her footsteps.

But she couldn't say any of that. So instead, she leaned back in her chair and lifted her gaze to the hair stylist, every bit the confident woman that she was. "Actually, I've never had my hair colored before. So I knew highlights were a thing, but I've not paid attention to how it's done. I've never had it done personally."

"Wow. Virgin hair. Donna, let me play with it."

Donna waved her off. "You're insane, Bette. If I allow you to get your hands on this pretty mane, Sophie'll leave here with her ends burned. No. We're treading lightly here."

Releasing a breath, Sophie offered Donna an appreciative smile. "Thank you. I'm a little nervous."

"I can tell. Your foot's tapping to a tune."

Sophie glanced down to find that, sure enough, her foot was tapping away on the tile floor. She lifted it up to the chair's footrest. "Sorry."

"It's fine, sweets. Hair is personal. As women, we define ourselves by our appearance, even those who claim they don't care. Even that is a look, you know?"

Sophie thought of Nana and thought that might not be true. Nana cared about God and Sophie and little else, certainly not makeup and nice clothes. Which was maybe why Sophie had always cared about them. She wasn't about to drop an arm and a leg on any of it, but she liked to look nice. It made her feel good, and she wouldn't apologize for that.

"It means a lot to me. My hair. I'm not really sure what I'd look like without my long blond hair. Like a stranger, I guess." Sophie laughed, but the thought settled uncomfortably over her. Was she really that defined by her looks? The busty blonde? Those were the two things he never spoke ill about, and over the years, those were the two things Sophie tried to maintain. But he wasn't a part of her identity anymore, and she'd made a pact with herself to think of her wants now—what she wanted, what she needed.

Well, this was the perfect opportunity to put her pact to the test and see if she could manage the business without being the busty blonde. She'd get these red-pink-whatever highlights and see if Rick at the grocery would still stock her produce. The risk made her contemplate telling Donna just to do the trim, she'd do the highlights next time—or in fifty years—but she was neck deep in this thing now. Literally. Because Donna had just snapped a cape around her neck and buttoned it, which felt a little too much like a straightjacket.

A shiver ran down her spine, but before she could dwell on it, the shop's door dinged and everyone's eyes cut over, including Sophie's. She tried with all her might to scrunch down in the chair and make herself invisible.

"Hiya, cute bottom. Whatcha doing here?" Donna asked Zac, a giant grin on her face. The same grin everyone wore around Zac because apparently he was a celebrity in Crestler's Key. Or maybe he really was a god. The thought made Sophie's stomach lurch.

He started to speak to Donna when his eyes cut down to Sophie. A wide, condescending smirk took over his face, stealing his original words.

"Well, well, Ms. Marsh. Wasn't expecting you here."

Sophie's eyes narrowed. "It's a salon."

"Ah, right. I guess you got me there." He strutted over and reached out to lift her hair. "Finally getting this cut?"

She swatted his hand away and flashed her best touch-me-again-and-I-will-break-this-hand-off glare. "And what exactly is that supposed to mean, Mr. Spike? Not everybody wears their hair gelled to high heaven."

The smirk returned, or maybe it'd never left. Sophie couldn't be sure. "You need to work on your insults. They don't land quite right. Maybe practice in front of a mirror. You know, while you're crying over this mistake you're about to make."

"Hey now." Donna play hit Zac in the stomach and then giggled as she ran her hand slowly down his abs before pulling away and murmuring something that sounded like "sweet Jesus." She headed to the back for more materials.

A horrified look crossed Zac's face, and Sophie burst into laughter that rumbled from her stomach to her toes. It felt good, and Sophie realized how rarely she laughed like that.

"You like that, now, do you? See, you're not the only one getting hit on around town."

"Is that what you call getting hit on? 'Cause if so, I'd say you need some help in the dating department. That was straight assault. You could call Jim and put in a restraining order, but that'd sure hurt your reputation around town."

Zac shrugged. "Nah, Donna's harmless."

"Yeah, probably."

"What about you?" he asked.

"What about me?"

He glanced around and then leaned closer, his arms bracing the chair on either side of her, his I-live-and-breathe-the-outdoors scent hitting her like a tall glass of iced tea after a long, hot day. "Are you harmless? Something tells me not so much."

"You know, you like to throw around stuff like that. Flirt and all. But I rarely see you with anyone around town. Having dating issues, Littleton?"

She expected him to laugh it off; after all, he looked like a freaking surfer, ripped body and all. What woman would turn down a man who looked like Zac? But instead of denying it, he stared down at Sophie like he couldn't quite figure her out and then pushed away as Donna neared.

"Whatcha doing here, sugar pants?" Donna asked.

First cute bottom, now sugar pants? Did all the women in town talk to Zac like this?

Probably so.

"Brought you some limes." He pointed to the front desk where a bag of bright green limes stared back at them.

Damn it. Sophie had hoped Donna got her produce from Rick's, not straight from the Littletons. Now she was going to be even harder to convert.

"Thank you, honey." Donna kissed his cheek, and Sophie realized for the first time that everyone here went around kissing cheeks. Once again, she thought she needed to adopt this skill if she wanted to fit in.

"All right, gotta hit the farm. See y'all ladies around." Zac winked at Sophie. "Until next time, Ms. Marsh."

Sophie crossed her arms, but then she realized he couldn't see that act of defiance beneath her cape and instead tried to fix him with that sure stare of hers. "Littleton."

He laughed as he turned around and started to put his aviator shades back in place, when he caught Annie-Jean by the front counter. "Annie-Jean, that you? I didn't recognize you with that cut."

The older woman beamed, and Zac walked over and, yep, pecked her cheek. "Had to try something different. I have me a new fella. You hear that?"

Zac smiled. "I did. You give him hell, Annie."

She winked. "You know it, honey."

Then Zac strutted out of the shop, those jeans of his showing off every tight contour of his backside. Gah. Sophie needed a man, stat.

Before she ran after the one she was supposed to hate.

Chapter Four

Zac parked his truck beside the U-Pick entrance and walked down to check out the strawberry patch. They'd start up that weekend, which was already two weeks late because of the late freeze this year.

As he approached, he saw plenty of red buried in the green and released the same breath he held every year until they were sure their crops would produce.

U-Pick was a monster all on its own. Separate from running the farm, Zac had to ensure U-Pick wasn't just about the berries in the spring or apples in the fall, but a full experience for the families that came there. Some traveled in for no other reason than to hit Littleton Farms U-Pick, and Zac couldn't let them leave disappointed. Sometimes he felt like he carried the weight of every customer's satisfaction, both the regulars' and those not yet discovered, on his shoulders.

He wondered if his brothers felt that same weight, but he suspected they didn't. Brady had never been the worrying sort, and when Charlie worried about something, he came to Zac.

"Hey, boss man," an aged voice called from behind him.

Zac pivoted around, a smile already forming, as he took in his father. Ned Littleton went gray at twenty-five and never looked back, but you would never guess his age by the look in his eyes, that yearning for life still sparkling like a star that refused to die. And he did refuse, given that he'd had two massive heart attacks and a run-in with skin cancer. The universe seemed to want Ned to bow his head in defeat or wave the white flag and accept that his time on Earth was over. But Ned refused to go quietly, and Zac suspected his father would kick and scream the entire way to the grave.

"What are you doing here? You know what Doc would say if he knew you were on the farm."

Ned winked. "Our little secret then."

"I'll keep it from Doc, but you're on your own with Mom."

Ned released a hearty laugh. "Wise man." Then he hobbled over with his cane to the first row of strawberries, peeled back the plastic, and took a good look. "Small this year."

"Yeah, I know. But they'll grow."

"Maybe." He hobbled around to the next row and peered down in the same way, continuing on to each of the ten rows they planted every year for the strawberry U-Pick season.

"What say you of that hippie naturalist grower in town? What's her name?"

Zac recovered the last row so his father wouldn't have to bend down, then faced Ned and squinted in the sun. "At Fresh Foods?" Even the mention of Sophie made Zac's insides come alive, which had to be his dislike of her and nothing more. But then he thought of his brothers accusing him of liking her and how frustrated he'd felt because maybe they were right.

"That's the one. Think they're cutting into our margins at all?"

With a shrug Zac motioned for Ned to follow him over to the other stations they had set up for the incoming crowd. The picnic tables for coloring or enjoying a piece of pie from the store. The playground and swing area. The petting zoo where baby chicks and goats and a few bunnies would be stationed for the kids to greet.

"Nah. I think eventually she might, but not yet. The town's not buying into the need to pay two or three times as much just to call it organic. But I'm trying a few more natural approaches to appease those who care."

Ned nodded. "That's a good idea."

"Thanks."

Ned stopped then and took a seat at one of the picnic tables. "You're doing a fine job, son. Real fine. Better than I could have ever hoped for. I just . . ." He ran a hand over his head, then glanced back up at Zac. "Well, I'm not sure I say it enough, but thank you. I know this wasn't what you wanted to do, that you'd rather—"

"I'm here because I want to be, Dad. And I won't have you thinking anything else about it."

But even as he said it, Zac turned away and adjusted the swings, one tangled up from the wind. Zac didn't want his father to see the flicker of disappointment that was sure to cross his face.

Zac loved his family, but Ned was right in his assumption that Zac never wanted to run the farm. But then, Zac didn't want to do a lot of things he found himself doing in adulthood. Juggling two businesses. Raising a daughter on his own. Avoiding dating for fear of alienating said daughter. The list could go on forever.

"I know you do what's right," Ned said. "That's what makes you the man you are. But just remember to take care of yourself, too. That's my one regret in life. Not doing what I wanted enough. Life's short—at least a few moments should be selfish."

Zac suspected this was a hard conversation for Ned to have, so he gave him the exit he needed. "I appreciate that. Well, I've got to go get Carrie-Anne ready."

"Where's she going?"

"Sleepover."

Ned whistled. "Wow. Getting big fast, isn't she?"

"Too fast."

"I'll let you get to it."

"Do you need a ride back to the house?"

"Nah, your mother will be by soon enough."

Zac hesitated, the idea of leaving his father alone unsettling, but hovering over the man who'd always been the strongest man Zac knew was even more unsettling.

As if he could read Zac's mind, Ned waved him on. "Go on now. Take care of my granddaughter. I'm fine."

"All right. See you later, Dad." He watched as his father focused on the farm, his eyes strained, and a pang of sadness worked through him.

Death might be easier than having to give up doing what you loved. Zac hoped he would never have to find out. So long as he could run both the farm and Southern Dive, he would keep doing it.

Now if only he could feel so certain about the other elements of his life.

Night set in faster than Zac cared for, and by nine thirty, he had already downed a couple of beers, surfed the TV in search of a game that apparently didn't exist, and called both of his brothers, who were out on dates. Because it was a Friday night, and that's what people did on Fridays.

Well, all people except him.

Zac tried to remember his last true date, and all he could come up with was a lunch with one of Kate's friends. Gemma? Jane? He could scarcely remember, having never been a name person. But what he did remember was the way she called him too quickly after the date. How she came by the farm, claiming to look for Kate, as though Kate had ever been a regular at the farm. And then she showed up at Brighton's Sandwich Shop, her eyes bright like she couldn't believe she was running into Zac. Again. And that was the end of that.

To be honest, he probably should have tried harder, but there was something about earning a woman's company, not simply asking for it and receiving it, that appealed to him. He hoped Carrie-Anne would make the boys beg for her attention, unlike all the foolish girls who posted on Instagram and Facebook in outfits and poses inappropriate for women twice their age, all in an effort to what? Get boys to notice them? Well, they likely did—but not in the way the girls hoped.

And now Zac had drifted into father mode. Again. He landed there more often than not these days, and he shuddered to think of what he'd become by the time Carrie-Anne went off to college.

What he needed was a distraction, a healthy or semi-unhealthy distraction that would tide over his brain until he could go to sleep without feeling like a boring old man. A distraction, a distraction— what could Zac do to pass time for a while? He thought back to the last time he'd been truly distracted, hell even entertained, and only one name came to mind—Sophie Marsh.

Hmm . . . Sophie Marsh.

The name kept creeping back into his life, much like the woman it belonged to, and Zac needed to end all thoughts of her before she and her name made a home in his head for good.

Grabbing the phone off the mount in the kitchen, Zac searched the call history until he found Sophie's number. He hit Call, not really sure what he would say when she picked up.

"Fancy hearing from you at nine thirty on a Friday night. Don't you get out?"

Zac grinned, the pressure in his chest easing. "Don't you?"

"Actually, I'm in mourning, so I have an excuse."

"Mourning?"

"You saw me at the salon."

A laugh broke free before Zac could tuck it away. "Now you have to send me a picture so I can see it. What are we talking about here? That pink stuff Donna puts in her daughter's hair, or did she just butcher it? Ah, damn, you're not sporting one of those boy cuts, are you?"

He could almost hear her cringing. "No, Mr. Chauvinistic. And besides, it's just hair."

"Right. And that's why you're stuck inside on a Friday night, probably staring at your reflection in the mirror in your bedroom, then the hall bathroom on the way to the kitchen, then doing it all over again, turning your head this way and that to see if you like it in different light." He couldn't keep the smile out of his voice. He'd seen Kate and his mother work through the same thing too many times growing up not to recognize the signs of a hair appointment gone horribly wrong. "I'm right, aren't I?"

"Shut up."

His grin spread, and for the briefest second, he thought he wouldn't be annoyed if Sophie were around more often just so he could spar with her. She brought out reactions in him that no one else did. Anger, sure, but there were other reactions. Reactions he didn't want to analyze right now.

"Why'd you do it anyway? Seems if a lady has good hair, she should leave it alone."

"Is there a compliment somewhere in that statement? I'm not good at deciphering bullshit from honesty."

Zac swallowed, unwilling to admit to as much, leaving the space open for her to talk so he could just listen and forget everything else for a while. "Trying to impress some guy in town?"

"Contrary to popular belief, not everything a woman does is for a man."

"All right, so what then? A bet? A run-in with the law and you needed an identity change?"

"You're ridiculous."

"Hey! No need for name calling. Just tell me."

"Why?"

"Why not?"

"Ugh! Fine. I'm trying to suck up to Donna, all right?"

That gave Zac pause. "Suck up to her? Why would you want to get in with Donna? Unless . . ." An uncomfortable feeling that felt a heck of a lot like disappointment settled over him. "Wow. I had no idea you were—"

"You can end that fantasy circling through that mush brain of yours right now. I wasn't trying to get-get with Donna."

"I believe that's two insults now. You're going to owe me dinner if you keep this up just so you can adequately say you're sorry."

"I'm not sorry."

"Not the point. You're supposed to say you're sorry to be polite."

"Says who?"

Zac leaned against the railing on his front porch, enjoying himself too much now to end the call. "Why'd they kick you out of Merryville again?"

"They didn't kick me out," she said, but Zac caught the break in her voice as she said it. There was definitely a story there, and he had every intention of uncovering it. But one thing at a time.

"So if you're not trying to get-get with Donna, then what are you trying to get from her?"

He could hear her tossing something around in aggravation, and he wished he were there so he could watch her feistiness taking shape, that petite thing so full of sass it was amazing she didn't grow a foot every time she lost her temper.

"Her business, okay?"

"Her hair business? Since when are you a hairstylist?"

"Ughhhhh. I'm not." She paused, and he suspected she was biting her tongue to keep from insulting him again. It made him want to push her even more. "I'm trying to get her lemon and lime business."

At that, he went silent, the urge to keep from laughing so strong that he feared if he breathed, the laugh would break free and she'd hang up on him. A good fifteen seconds of silence passed before he trusted himself enough to speak.

"You realize she gets maybe a bag every two weeks, right? That's like, what? Five bucks of that expensive stuff you sell? You hurting that badly, Marsh, that you gotta swindle away five dollars? Look, I'll save you the trouble and bring over a five right now. Make you feel better and all."

"God, you really are insufferable."

Zac grinned as he lay back in the porch swing and let it sway back and forth, the night peaceful, not a cloud in the sky to block the stars. "Thank you. I try."

"Gah, see that. You are horrible!" She hesitated, then added, "Ugh, wait. I'm sorry. I'm not normally such a mean person, but you make me want to—"

"Scream? You know, I'd love to test that response in other areas."

"Are you this ridiculous with everyone, or do I get that prize all to myself?"

He thought about it, and surprisingly, he couldn't think of another woman who he liked to jab at like Sophie. At first, it was the competition between them, especially on market days. But there was something else there, too. He enjoyed her reactions, the way her lips pursed in aggravation every time she saw him. It made him want to push her buttons a little bit more to see if she'd pop. Which was mean as hell, but fun all the same. Still, he had no intention of admitting that to her.

"Now, now, you wouldn't think you're that special, would you?"

"Look, I—"

"Back to Donna. So you screwed up your hair to try to get her business?"

"Not just hers. All those ladies that hang around her salon. Donna let me leave some pens and magnets because I spent like two hundred dollars on a cut and highlights and lowlights and shampoo and conditioner and hair volumizer and some pomade crap that scares me to even think about putting in my hair. And yet, I didn't even get to talk to the other ladies. They hate me."

"They don't hate you."

"They don't like me."

"I, well . . ." Zac dropped a foot to the ground and pushed, causing the swing to move again.

"You can admit it. I know they don't. I just don't know what I did? I'm nice, right?"

Zac laughed, and Sophie growled into the phone. "I was about to say yes. It was on the tip of my tongue."

"Sure you were. I just don't know what to do. If I can't get them to like me, they'll never buy from me. I need . . . oh my God. Why didn't I think of this before?"

Zac glanced around as though she were there and had picked up on something he hadn't. "Um, not following you here."

"Are you at home? Wait, that was a stupid question. Of course you are. You called me from your landline. Come to think of it, why did you call?"

He released a slow breath. "I . . . I don't really know."

"But you're not going anywhere right now, right?"

"Probably not. What are you—" He heard the dial tone, and he eyed the phone, unsure what the hell had just happened. Clearly, Sophie was this side of crazy, and he needed to get said crazy person out of his mind. Right now.

He drew a breath and released, cleared his mind. There, see? Done. Gone.

Twirling the phone around in his hand, he stared at the keypad, curious if he should call her back. Maybe she'd accidentally hung up, or he had, and she was waiting on him to call back.

And now he sounded like a chick. Freaking hell.

Resigned that he needed to find something to do, he hit the shower and then put on pajama pants and double-checked that he had everything set up for the next few dive classes at Southern Dive.

Everything was all set. He'd killed twenty minutes, and yet he ached to call Sophie back. He had just opened his laptop and sat down in his dark leather recliner to research new equipment for the farm when he heard a knock at the door.

Sure that it was Carrie-Anne, homesick, he raced to the door, prepared to baby her the way he was known for doing. Instead, he opened the door and stared straight into the clear blue eyes of someone else—Sophie.

Her hair flowed down her back and shoulders in long blond and strawberry waves, like it had been kissed by the sun itself. Her face was bare, so the tiny brown beauty mark on her right cheek stood out. She wore baggy jeans with a hole in the knee, a white tank top, and flip-flops—this Sophie in such sharp contrast to the one he was used to seeing that he did a double take.

His mouth fell slack, his mind shutting down, and only one word came to mind. "Wow."

"Are you going to let me in or keep staring at me like a fool?"

Fool sounded about right.

Chapter Five

"I know. I look like a freaking Bratz doll. And I'm sorry about this." Sophie swirled a finger in front of her face. "Had to get over here, and I'd already taken off my makeup. I'm a total raccoon, but I assure you it's me."

Her brows threaded together, and she contemplated covering her face with her hair, but it was a hot mess, too, thanks to Donna. "Look, I get that I look crazy, but seriously? I'm not an alien or anything. Why are you staring at me like that?"

Zac jerked back like he'd finally snapped back to reality, then he cleared his throat and looked away.

"Oh my God." Suddenly Sophie realized that she'd walked in on Zac Littleton in his home, at night, and he was dressed for the hour. His hair was still wet from a recent shower, and beyond a pair of low-hanging plaid pajama pants that showed off the deep V of his pelvic muscle, he was naked. Naked except for a thin pair of pajama pants. Heaven above . . .

Now it was Sophie's turn to stare. "Wow."

"Yeah, that's what I said."

"No, I'm talking about you." Sophie pointed at him, unable to hide her thoughts. "I didn't know you had so many tattoos. Or so many muscles."

Zac glanced down at his bare chest, and Sophie took that as an invitation for her to do the same. Wow didn't even cover it.

She knew Zac was fit, but nothing like this. This? This was magazine worthy—drool worthy. Cut muscle after cut muscle, wish-she-could-stroke-his-abs worthy. Now she understood why Donna had thrown out a "Sweet Jesus" after she touched Zac's stomach at the salon. Sophie was close to mumbling her own *sweet Jesus*, and she hadn't even touched him.

Clearing her throat, she glanced away before she embarrassed herself.

"What are you doing?"

She covered her eyes to keep the devils from wandering. "Letting you get dressed."

"I am dressed."

"You know, the rest of the way. With a shirt."

"Look, lady, you came to my house. This is what I look like at my house at ten forty-five at night."

Steeling herself for the sight of those abs again, Sophie forced herself to face him and lift her head a touch higher. "Where's Carrie-Anne?"

"At a friend's tonight."

Sophie caught the way he glanced at his cellphone as he said it, the hint of worry around his eyes. "First sleepover?"

"Yeah, first one not with my parents or Kate."

"She'll be fine."

"Yeah," Zac said, running a hand through his hair that caused the wet strands to stick out in the most adorable way. And . . . craptastic. She needed to get her head on straight if she had any hope of doing what she came here to do. "She's not the problem."

A pinch of understanding worked through Sophie's heart. "Ah, growing up too fast?"

"So fast. It feels like she was just learning to walk yesterday, and now she's talking about lip gloss and sleepovers and God knows what else when I'm not around."

"She's a good girl, Zac. You raised her well."

His eyes met hers for the first time since he opened the door. "I hope so. Feels like you can only do so much, and then you have to hope the groundwork you built over all those years stands up to the pressures they'll face, ya know?"

She nodded, though she didn't really know at all. By now, she had hoped to have children, but *he* didn't want children, so she . . .

She trailed off before her thoughts went any darker. That was in the past, where it would remain.

"Anyway, enough dad drama. I thought you hung up on me."

Sophie cocked her head, her lips twitching at the corners. "You sound disappointed."

"What can I say? I enjoy fighting with you." He winked, and Sophie felt her neck burn. She couldn't have this conversation with Zac when he was standing there in next to no clothes, looking like that. Seriously? What sane woman could have any conversation at all?

"Can you put on a shirt?"

That arrogant grin of his flashed on his face, and he crossed his arms, flexing his biceps in an I-know-what-I'm-doing-to-you-and-I-like-it way. Sophie swallowed hard.

"You know, I don't think so. Seems I need an upper hand around you. This seems to give me that margin, but if it'd make you feel better, you can remove your shirt so we're on the same playing field again. I won't be offended in the least."

Her eyes narrowed, zeroing in, before she shook her head. "Never mind. I don't know what I was thinking coming here. You're such an arrogant ass muncher."

Zac grabbed her arm just before she made it to the door and peered down at her. His clean, all-outdoors scent washed over her.

"Ass muncher."

"You deserved it."

"I did. And I'm sorry. Don't leave. I'll be good."

She cocked her head.

"And I'll put on a shirt."

"Good. I'll just wait here."

"See, we're getting along better already." Zac tossed her a crooked grin before disappearing down a long hallway.

Sophie took the opportunity to examine his house. She'd never been there before, but if she could have guessed what it would look like, she would have guessed this.

The walls were a warm caramel throughout, and the family room had been decorated with a dark leather couch and two recliners, a few photos on the wall. It was an open floor plan, the granite-and-stone kitchen visible from the family room, the dining room with rustic furnishings to its left. She wondered if his mother had helped decorate or maybe Kate or if he'd done it all on his own. There was a cozy vibe, but also something decidedly male about it. She wondered if he allowed Carrie-Anne to paint her room pink or if he had blanched at the idea. She wondered a lot of things about Zac Littleton, and she found each detail she discovered only made her desperate for more.

"Better?"

She turned to find him in a basic white T and the same pajama pants as before, barefoot.

"You didn't say the PJs were an issue."

"They aren't . . . so long as they stay in place."

Zac broke into laughter. "Contrary to popular belief, I don't drop my pants every chance I get. You're safe with me."

"I know that."

Their eyes locked for a second, and Sophie noticed brown flecks within his green irises. His tongue wet his bottom lip, and he swallowed, causing his Adam's apple to bob. Sophie took a step back, needing space from the energy bouncing between them.

"So, I'm just going to get on with it."

"Please do."

"I came here to make a truce." She peered at him for his reaction.

His eyebrows lifted. "A truce."

"Or something. Whatever the word is. I need your help, and I'm betting there's something I could offer you in return." Then she pointed at him before that dirty mind of his could explore. "And not *that* kind of offer in return."

He threw up his hands, but he was smiling. "Hey, I didn't say anything."

"You were thinking it."

"I'll never admit a thing."

Sophie shook her head, but she smiled as her gaze met his again. "I need the town to like me, at least a little, and they love you. So I thought maybe you could help me. Maybe we could go to lunch from time to time or something, act like we're friends. Show them you like me, so maybe they will, too."

"You're asking me to help you steal my business? I don't think so, sweetheart. I might not be the sharpest tool in the shed, but I'm not an idiot either."

"No, not your business. Just the little stuff. With some of the women around town, stuff that would work for me that you aren't really handling. Like AJ&P."

"I cover AJ&P."

"I know, but you don't grow cherries, oranges, or raspberries. Let me have that business. Just the stuff you don't grow."

She could see that he was considering it, a tiny thread holding him there, and she needed to tighten its hold around him before he took a step back and broke the connection. "Please. I'll help you do something, too. Maybe convert part of your farm to organic. Could only help you."

Zac shook his head. "Got that already covered, thanks. I don't think there's anything I need."

"You have to. Everyone needs something. Maybe something for Carrie-Anne. Something she wants? I could help her with makeup or nails or something. Think of something she wants that you aren't giving her and I could help."

Zac turned away then, like he'd thought of that very thing already but wasn't so sure he wanted to ask. Or maybe he didn't trust Carrie-Anne with her, which made her sad. Because she really was a nice person. Really.

"You could be there for the makeup stuff of course, if you wanted. I know you don't know me well enough maybe to trust your daughter with me, but—"

"I trust you. It's not that."

"But there *is* something?"

He faced her then, his top teeth clamped down over his bottom lip, his eyes squinted in thought, those strong arms of his crossed again. Sophie wished she could ask him to relax his arms at his sides so she could focus, because damn. But before she could contemplate how to talk to him without staring at his biceps, he said, "No, never mind."

"What? Just tell me. I'll do it, anything. I need to make a home here. I need it. You have no idea how badly I need this."

With new interest, Zac studied her, a thousand questions in his eyes. But even if she wanted Zac's help, she wouldn't tell him the real reason she'd moved to Crestler's Key. No one could know.

"What do you need me to do?" she asked again.

Zac drew a long breath, and then the words tumbled out in what sounded like a long, exhausted sigh. "Carrie wants me to date, wants to see that I'm at least trying. Her friend Reagan's mom said something and . . . I don't know." He ran a hand through his hair and peeked over at her again. "This sounds crazy."

"You dating? Not crazy at all actually. I could fix you up with someone. Oh! Maybe Glenda."

"Actually, I was thinking we could kill two birds with one stone."

Sophie froze. "What do you mean?"

For a beat, Zac didn't say anything, and Sophie feared he'd backtrack again, when instead he took a step toward her. "You need the town to like you, and I need my daughter to trust that I'm okay. So we pretend to date. Carrie feels better because I'm not alone here all the time, so she doesn't feel guilty when she leaves, and you get some good-faith points with the town. Two problems, one solution. Done."

Now it was Sophie's turn to laugh. "Pretend to date. Us? We hate each other. You've got to be out of your mind."

Zac shrugged. "Maybe. But seems it would take care of both of our problems. We hang out—nothing too serious so Carrie doesn't grow attached. I couldn't have that. Just a little light dating, show the town we're friendly, make my daughter feel better, and then after a few months, we can stop it. No big deal."

"You're serious."

"Dead. I don't want to risk women coming around here all the time, getting too attached, and messing with Carrie's life and well-being. This way, I control it. And it helps your case with the town. Win-win."

Sophie turned away, the remnants of a laugh still on the verge of spilling over. He couldn't be serious. Couldn't be. Yet as she glanced back at him, studied his expression, the sincerity in his eyes, she could see that he was absolutely serious.

"Okay, let's say for argument's sake that I consider this. How would it work? Would we set rules? Like no dating anyone else or something?"

"Neither of us is dating anyone else anyway."

That stung, but Sophie couldn't deny it. "True."

"So it's settled then?"

Sophie bit her thumbnail and met his gaze again. "No physical stuff."

"Of course. Except, you know, the basics."

"The basics?"

Zac took a step toward her and reached out his hand as though it were the most natural thing in the world, then linked his fingers through hers. "This."

Sophie stared down at their interlocked fingers, curious what the tingly feeling working up those fingers and into her arm was all about. Maybe she was just tired. "And what about kissing."

Their eyes locked.

"What about it?"

"Should we, you know, kiss? On occasion? Just to keep up pretenses of course."

Zac considered it, stared off into his kitchen, then at a photo over his fireplace, before regarding her with something like uncertainty. "We'll take that as it comes."

Sophie nodded, her belly flipping and flopping with thoughts of Zac's full lips on hers, those strong arms around her, securing her to him. Lord Almighty, she might not survive fake dating Zac Littleton if kissing was involved.

"Is that nod a yes?"

"Something tells me I don't have much of a choice."

"With me, you always have a choice. Despite what you think, I'm not a bad guy."

Sophie tried to swallow the lump forming in her throat. "I'm starting to see that."

"So, dating?"

"I'll agree to a few dates."

"A few dates?" Zac scratched his chin and flashed her one of those warm smiles that promised sweet dreams and happily-ever-afters. Things Sophie would never know. But maybe for a few weeks, she could pretend that a life with a man like Zac was possible.

"A few dates."

"I can work with that."

Chapter Six

The smell of apples and cinnamon filled the air, powdered sugar dotted Sophie's dress in three spots, the scene reminiscent of happy, bubbly times, and yet she still couldn't pull her mind away from Zac and their agreement. And whether she'd made an epic mistake.

For one, it had been four days since she had spoken with him. Four long days without a word. If this was the way Zac Littleton dated a woman, then it was understandable why he struggled to get a date. And maybe that was why he offered this agreement in the first place. Maybe he hated dating and preferred to just screw around, but didn't—couldn't—say as much to his daughter, so he needed to fake date Sophie so he could continue his shadowy escapades, all the while the town would know he was cheating on Sophie. And maybe he'd even get one of these escapade-ers pregnant, and then the whole town would think Sophie was a fool. But then maybe—

"You've been quiet."

Sophie glanced over at Glenda, who pulled another pie from the oven and placed it on the cooling rack with the others. Apple. Peach. Blueberry. Each a different recipe that Nana had taught her all those years ago when she would visit, stand on the stool Papa had made, and watch in awe as Nana turned powder to pie.

What would Nana say if she knew about this plan Sophie had agreed to, all in an effort to secure more business. There was a certain ickiness to it that made her want to call Zac and say she had changed her mind. But then, if she were honest, really honest, she was curious about what spending more time with Zac looked like. What it felt like. How he might act when she was supposed to be his date instead of his enemy. Would he still produce that sexy, annoy-

ing smirk of his, like any second he might laugh at her . . . or would
he sweep her into his arms and press his lips to hers and—

Get a hold of yourself!

"Earth to Sophie."

"What? Oh, yeah. I know, I'm sorry. I have a lot on my mind."

"Like?"

Like tall, tattooed farmers.

"Nothing really."

Glenda pulled off her oven mitts and walked around to where Sophie was dropping lemon tarts into cellophane bags. "I'm your friend."

"I know. Kind of hard to forget the only one I have," Sophie said
with a little laugh that sounded an awful lot like a little cry.

"They'll come around."

Sophie shrugged and dropped three more tarts into the bags, tied
a ribbon and a Fresh Foods daisy logo tag onto each. She might not
be the best baker in town or the number-one farmer in town, but no
one could argue with her presentation.

And yet, presentation did not pay bills.

"See that's actually part of the problem. I don't know if they will
come around, which is why I really don't have a choice, right? I
mean, it's my business and I need to do something, or else it's going
to completely fail, and I can't fail at this. I need to stay here and succeed. But how can I succeed if no one trusts me, which is really why
there's only one thing to do. And I'm committed. And—"

"Soph," Glenda said, patting her hand. "I love you. But I have absolutely no idea what you're talking about. So let's back up a taste
and start again. What do you mean you have no choice? No choice
about what?"

Clenching her eyes tight, Sophie drew a breath for courage and
released it, the words spilling out before she told the whole damn
town and ruined everything even before they started. "I'm pretending to date Zac Littleton so the town will like me." She pressed her
hands to her face, smearing more powdered sugar in her Bratz doll
hair, which she still wasn't used to but couldn't do a thing about. "I
know what you're thinking. I'm crazy and it's stupid and I don't
even know how I got myself into this, but I think—"

"I think it's genius!"

Peeling her eyelids open, Sophie peeked over at her friend.
Maybe she was insane, too. "Seriously? You think it's a good idea?"

"No, I think it's the best thing I've ever heard, certainly the best idea you've come up with. He's the quintessential town golden child, and you're the black sheep. Mix the two together?" She clapped her hands like she was forcing the two to become one, which felt a little like what they were doing. "It's like a black-and-white cookie or marble cake—total perfection. They'll love you by default, trust you by default. And then they'll buy your stuff to support you because you're one of them. I love it!"

Sophie wrinkled her nose. "Yeah, but isn't that deceptive? I mean, what happens when we fake break up? They hate me again?"

"Oh, you'll have to make it so he dumps you. That's the only way it'll work. He'll rebound fine because he's homegrown and all, but you? If you ended it? You'd become the town pariah, and we can't have that. So make sure he dumps you. Preferably in a public place like AJ&P Bakery or the market or something."

"This is crazy."

"Crazy awesome. I'm so excited!" Glenda's eyebrow lifted, and she smiled like Sophie had just announced her engagement. "Whose idea was it anyway?"

This was still the hardest part for Sophie to digest. "Zac's. I went there to ask him to kind of be my friend around town a little, and he basically said what's in it for him, and I said anything—you know, shy of sexual favors. And he said he had something, and now here we are."

"Wait—you took sexual favors off the table? Have you seen his body?"

"Actually, yeah. When I went there, he was wearing pajama pants and nothing else."

Glenda dropped the pie she'd been holding, and Sophie tossed her hands. "Well that's ten bucks down the drain."

"I'm sorry. My mind locked on Zac Littleton with no clothes on, and it short-circuited. Damn, how big was it?"

"Dear God, my best friend is a sixteen-year-old in a woman's body. I didn't say he was naked. He was wearing pajama pants."

"Oy. Missed that part. But the rest must have been a sight to see, huh?"

Sophie thought back to his bulging pecs, his rippled abs, that defined V of his pelvic muscle, and then the dark trickle of hair that trailed from his navel down into his pajama pants. "Yeah..." she said with a sigh that aggravated her more than it should have. She was a living, breathing woman with working vision. Of course she found Zac attractive. She'd have to be blind not to, and even that wouldn't stop her with that rugged, deep voice of his. The more she thought about it, the more dangerous this little agreement became.

"So no sex?"

"Um, well . . . we didn't really talk about that."

Glenda scooted closer. "So sex isn't off the table? That's the best thing I've heard all day. And what about other stuff?"

"We're just pretending. It's not like that."

"But it could be like that. If you wanted it to be, right?"

Sophie let that idea settle over her before shaking it from her mind. "No. I'm probably going to tell him I can't do it anyway. It feels too dishonest."

"Not dishonest, just a little marketing with the town's preferred product."

A little marketing. Hmm, saying it like that made it seem less horrific in Sophie's mind. "Maybe . . ."

Just then the door opened to the Fresh Foods store, located at the entrance of her farm, where she sold her baked goods and had fresh produce ready for customers to grab what they needed and head on their way.

Sophie expected one of her regulars to walk through the door, but instead she watched as a frantic Annie-Jean Carlisle rushed toward her.

"Hey there, honey. I heard you had a solid supply of Granny Smiths?"

"Me?" Sophie glanced around, sure Annie had stumbled into the wrong store. "Here?"

Annie quirked an eyebrow at her. "Yes, you. You're the one standing there, aren't you?"

"But I thought you bought from Zac?"

"I do. But he's out, and he sent me here, and I have a huge order for turnovers due tomorrow, so if you don't have them, then I'll need to head to Lexington, and I hate that drive. So Granny Smiths or no, dear?"

Sophie's brain had stopped working at Zac sent her. Zac. So he was serious—they were doing this. Wow.

"Honey, I'm old, and my time is like gold. Either show me to the apples or to the door. I've got orders to fill."

"Right, right. Sorry." Sophie clapped her hands together loudly, which caused both women to stare at her like she'd lost a few marbles. She swallowed hard and forced herself to appear less spazzy. "They're right here." She walked to the far left side of the store to the stand full of vibrant green apples. "And we have more if you need them."

"I do. I'll take all of this and then five more bags. Do you sell them by the bag or crate?"

Sophie's head spun as she tried to process what Annie had said. "Did you just say all of them? As in, all of them?"

"Yes, dear. Do you have hearing problems, because if so, I can recommend a good ear doctor in Triple Run. Otherwise, I'll just take my apples please."

Sophie reached forward and hugged Annie-Jean before she could stop herself. "Thank you. That's just . . . thank you!"

Annie-Jean extracted herself from Sophie's hold with a worried look on her face. "You're not in Doc Sanders's care, are you?"

"Me? Oh no."

"'Cause I don't really do business with anyone under his care. Risk and all."

"Of course."

Sophie continued to stare at Annie-Jean, who looked at her as though she'd lost her mind.

"The apples."

"Oh! Right." Scooting off to the back before she said or did anything else embarrassing, Sophie pulled down crates from her shelves to box up the apples.

"So . . . you're going for scary, huggy lady as your tactic to get the town to like you?" Glenda asked as she reached for another crate.

"I know. God. I just freaked out. She's taking them all. Like, every one of them."

"I heard her. So Zac did this? No way is he actually out of apples. He runs an orchard, for Christ's sake."

Sophie considered that for a second. "You're right. He sent her here to help me."

"Now it's time you help him." Glenda waggled her eyebrows, and Sophie bit her lip.

"Yeah, I guess it is."

They came back out with the crates and together packaged everything up, then helped Annie-Jean carry it all to the AJ&P van she had parked outside. Finally, when they had everything packed in the van, Sophie beamed at Annie-Jean.

"Thank you again. Truly." She leaned in to kiss Annie-Jean's cheek, but Annie jerked back.

"Um, you're welcome." She shook her head as she slid into the driver's seat and peeled away.

"Smooth. Now your one and only new customer thinks you're hitting on her."

Sophie laughed as she covered her face with her hands. "Oh my God, she so does." She giggled still harder, but she was too happy to be embarrassed now.

"But freaky behavior aside, we've been open for fifteen minutes, and we've already hit our daily sales goal."

Sophie's grin returned. "I could get used to this." Then she headed toward the store.

"Where are you going?"

She winked over her shoulder. "To set up my first date with Zac Littleton."

Zac couldn't stop smiling. Which was a problem, really, because he was poring over the farm's financials, and there was nothing there worth smiling about.

But Annie had called him twenty minutes earlier to recount her trip to Fresh Foods at Zac's insistence and to ask why Sophie both hugged her and tried to kiss her and whether that meant she swung a certain way. Which, according to Annie, was perfectly fine—she thought marriage should be open to whoever the hell was stupid enough to go down that road—but she was too old for Sophie. And far too straight.

It'd taken him a half hour on the phone to convince Annie that Sophie was as straight as she was; Sophie was just showing her appreciation for the business and being nice, and since when did anyone in Crestler's Key have an issue with hugging?

When Annie asked exactly how he knew of her sexual preferences, he had to close his mouth and think on that. Because the truth of it was that no woman interested in women would gawk at him shirtless the way Sophie had last night. There had been a change in the air, some unspoken attraction passing between them that had maybe always been there but neither had been willing to set free until that moment.

And now he couldn't for the life of him rein it back in.

Now, an affronted Sophie, all wide eyes and round mouth, kept circling through his mind. With the number of hugs given out in this town, Sophie must have been shocked when Annie pulled away. Hell, even Zac was surprised at Annie, but this was Annie-Jean Carlisle, and though she liked to pretend to be a radical, she was as partial to locals as the rest of them.

Zac peered back at his laptop, the email he'd received from the farm's accountant still open and all the horridness of the winter season there for him to see. U-Pick would speed up their financial recovery, but each year they needed a little more than the year before to survive. With the late freeze, Zac feared U-Pick wouldn't turn the profit they needed, and the farm would go negative for the first time ever.

The pressure of it hit him in the chest, radiating to his left shoulder, and he rubbed the spot until it eased. Not for the first time, he worried that heart attacks were genetic and he was bound to suffer one any second. From stress, if nothing else.

Shaking off the thought, he leaned back in his leather desk chair and closed his eyes, trying to think positive thoughts because hell if negative ones did anything but make him feel worse. He'd just decided to call his brothers to talk it over when his cell vibrated against the desk, an unknown number flashing across the screen.

Never one to trust a number he didn't know on his cellphone, he sent the call to voicemail and went back to his accountant's document to search for a trend that they could monitor and improve upon. A few seconds passed, and the phone began to vibrate again, the same number flashing. Once again, he sent it to voicemail, a tinge of aggravation creeping up. What the hell? Was the telemarketer required to hear a voice before he or she could back off and move on to the next poor sap?

When a minute passed without another call, Zac thought the caller had moved on, but the phone began to vibrate again, this time the sound so loud in the otherwise silent office that Zac contemplated tossing his phone across the room, but he couldn't do that. Wouldn't do that. Zac was a lot of things, but explosive wasn't one of them. That had always been Lora's job. She was the yeller, not Zac.

He thought back to when they first began dating, how she would smile at anything, how her laugh was infectious, causing him and anyone around them to laugh, too. They were married six months later, which, looking back, could have been part of the problem—they didn't really know one another. Yet those first few years were happy. Or at least they weren't unhappy. No, the unhappy days and months and years showed their ugly heads later.

Lora would find some fault in everything, every moment and action. He could do nothing right. His tics, which used to make her grin, soon led to snide comments, then arguments so intense that Zac would have no choice but to shake his head and walk away. By that point, Zac had dedicated himself to his coaching job at the school and his new baby girl. He couldn't imagine leaving Lora, even if she would scream at him to leave so often he'd been tempted to toss up his hands and say, "Fine. I'm out." But Zac wasn't a quitter, not in life and certainly not with his family.

Maybe that was why he'd been blind to her affair, why he never thought she would actually leave. Because *he* never would have left. Months after he watched her walk away, he wondered if he'd picked up his socks, if he'd placed the cap back on the toothpaste, if he'd tried a little harder, would she have stayed? But then he realized he deserved someone who wanted to stay in spite of his faults. Someone who loved him and Carrie-Anne so much that nothing could drive her away, and that person wasn't Lora.

Now, he drew a breath to bring himself back to the moment, but instead of tossing the phone across the room like he wanted to do, he answered the call and immediately let the telemarketer have it.

"Look, I get it. You're on some hourly bonus structure, and you've got to land a few callers to even make this job seem worth it. But I'll tell you a secret—it will never be worth it. This is junk work, and you have to decide—either that's fine or it's not. But I'm not your guy today I don't need knives or a new vacuum. I can't donate any more money to the children who need water in wherever. I'm tapped out. And despite how that sounds, I'm not a jerk. I'm just responsible, and even the most giving people know that it's about balance. So just call someone else, or better yet, I'll give you twenty to *not* call the next person. Give that poor person a break for the day. How's that sound? Let me know when you're ready for my card number."

But instead of a monotone voice on the other end, his request was met with barely contained laughter. He closed his eyes as a strange relief washed over him.

"Whoa, that was something else," Sophie said, her voice light.

"All right, then, have your fun. Laugh away."

"I am. Loudly. Come to think of it, I might have just alarmed the neighbors. Oh wait, you're the neighbor. Can you hear me laughing way over there at Littleton Farms?"

"You're hysterical."

"And you're crazy, but I guess we all have problems. Man, that was like a look into one of your psych sessions or something. Do you always go off on telemarketers like that, or did I just strike you at the wrong time? And can I have that twenty you promised? I won't call Glenda next if that helps secure it."

"You know, I'm regretting helping you more and more each second."

At that the laughter died down, but he could still hear the smile in her voice, and he'd be lying if he said he wasn't enjoying himself. "Fine. I'm done."

"Great."

"So thank you for helping me today. Whatever you did—that lie, whatever—to get Annie-Jean over here. She bought every green apple I had, probably a few red ones, too. Kind of hated me a bit as she did it, but still, it was amazing. And so, okay."

Zac sat forward and propped his elbows up on the desk that had once been his father's and in his head always would be. "Okay what?"

"Okay, you proved you'll keep your end of our little agreement. So will I. How's tonight?"

"How's tonight for what? I'm starting to think I'd rather you'd been the telemarketer after all. At least then I'd have given my money and been done with it."

"How much money do these people guilt you into giving them? You know they do that on purpose."

"Which part?"

"All of it. I used to make calls for my college when I was a sophomore and couldn't afford to eat anything but ramen and peanut butter. Took that job and discovered that those people keep a file from here to Alaska on everything they've ever picked up about you. Where you work, your interests, your family, the exact thing said during the last call that made you pony up. Though I guess in this case, the telemarketer would have written, *said nothing, called a crazy person.*"

"Ha ha."

She giggled again, and Zac contemplated asking her not to say anything else for a minute so he could hold onto the sound for a bit longer. He wasn't sure why he loved her laugh so much or when exactly he had started loving it, but there was a pureness to the sound, a freedom that made Zac wish his laughs felt the way hers sounded.

"So, as I was saying—how's tonight?"

"Um, cloudy with a chance of rain? I have no idea what you're asking me."

"The dating thing. God. Do you need it spelled out for you? You said to help me around town I had to date you. So I am. Now, again, slower this time—hooow iiiiis toniiiiiiiigggght?"

"You want to go out tonight."

"Might as well get this show started."

"Do you realize you speak in expressions, or do they just pour out of you?"

"Guess you'll have to find out tonight. Want me to pick you up? How's seven?"

"Wait, no. I can pick you up. It's—"

"Don't tell me you're into that male chauvinistic crap, where a man has to do all the male things and a woman has to do all the woman things?"

"I didn't say that, but—"

"Then it's settled." A jingle hit his ears, and Sophie called out a hello. "Gotta run, have a customer. See you at seven, lover." And then she hung up, Zac's head still reeling from whatever the hell had just happened.

He closed his laptop and leaned back in his chair, excitement coursing through him as he glanced down at his watch. Three hours and counting until he went on his first date with Sophie.

Chapter Seven

Sophie stared at her reflection in her bedroom vanity and reached a hand out to glide over the aged mirror, her mind thinking back to watching Nana brush her long white hair before the very same mirror. She ached to go see Nana now and decided to pop over to the nursing home where she lived tomorrow.

Nana had developed Alzheimer's three years ago, and for a year, Sophie tried to manage it on her own. Then she hired someone to stay at the house with them, but soon she realized Nana's care demanded more attention and more trained professionals. It had broken Sophie into pieces to walk away from Nana at the nursing home, to listen as she screamed for Sophie to come back, to not abandon her. Sophie barely made it to her car before she burst into tears.

But soon Nana's fragile memory forgot Sophie entirely. Forgot that her daughter even had a daughter. To Nana, Sophie's mother was still a teenager, too beautiful for her own good and bringing Nana more heartache and headache than any parent should have to suffer.

For a while, Sophie could go see Nana without upsetting her, but the truth was, Sophie looked so much like her mother that Nana would often fall into some old memory and end up crying or yelling. And if Sophie tried to be herself, Nana would grow frightened and confused, which always led to intervention from one of the nursing home staff.

So it had taken Sophie a long time to come to terms with the fact that she was more harm than good when it came to Nana, and the best she could do was check in on her from a distance—visits without actually saying anything other than a hello, never hugging her or kissing her wrinkled cheek. It ripped the tear in her heart a little bit more every time she visited, but she couldn't bring herself to not go at all. Not going felt like abandonment, and even if Nana didn't know Sophie, she still needed someone who knew her and loved her.

But now, as she ran a hand down her long waves, the layers Donna had put in to keep her fine hair fuller, Sophie wondered what Nana would say about her dating Zac Littleton just to grow her business. Would she approve like Glenda? Or would she shake her head in shame. The crappy part about it was that Sophie's motives weren't simple, which made her feel both better and worse.

Sure, she wanted the town to like her, but what she really wanted was for them to like her for her, not because of her association with Zac. It hurt to think that they didn't like her, because Sophie was a nice, caring person. So why didn't they like her?

The whole thing brought back all those feelings of inadequacy from when she was a kid, her on the swings watching all the other girls chasing after the boys or playing princesses, but never allowing Sophie to play. She was a tiny thing back then, with crooked teeth that probably looked a little yellow because at seven she'd never been to the dentist, and clothes that were always a little too short or tight or had holes in them that she couldn't hide. She wore sandals long past warm weather because her sneakers would be too small and hurt her feet. Her father was a police officer who'd been shot and killed during a drug raid, and it'd torn her mother apart.

Sophie was five years old when it happened, and although her mother wasn't an evil person, she wasn't exactly good either. She didn't hit Sophie or drink or allow random men in the house. She just didn't love her. Or at least not as much as she loved herself. Nana would send money all the time, but that money never trickled down to Sophie or her needs. Eventually, Nana started buying Sophie things instead of providing money, always asking what she needed— school supplies or new shoes. Nana never bought anything fancy, but when Sophie was used to wearing things that didn't fit, clothes from Wal-Mart felt like luxury.

Sophie probably had her mother to blame for her love of fashion—shoes, clothes, accessories. But the difference between Sophie and her mother was that Sophie refused to go into debt over these things, and she certainly wouldn't allow her child to go without so she could get a new handbag. People acted like there were only a handful of true addictions in the world—drugs, alcohol, sex, whatever. But Sophie knew better.

An addiction was anything a person couldn't step away from, anything that hindered her ability to handle the responsibilities of her life. And Sophie's mother's addiction had been shopping.

Shaking off the thought before she became bitter, Sophie stood and peered at her simple, flowy tank dress; the teal tone of the dress paired with pink and ivory jewelry had a decidedly feminine vibe that made Sophie smile. The fact that she'd scored the jewelry at the market in Charleston, handmade and for only ten bucks, made her even happier.

Hopefully Zac will like it.

But even as the thought hit her, Sophie's eyes went wide, and she pointed at her reflection. "Oh, no, missy. None of that business here. You keep this casual, understand? Ignore the force!"

And now she was talking to herself.

But she couldn't help it. It'd been a long time since Sophie had gone on a date, and though this wasn't real, it felt real. She had that swirly butterfly feeling in her stomach. Her hands kept going clammy, despite her washing those suckers two or three times to try to rinse away the panic. That nervous first date feeling was there, a reality, enough that Sophie contemplated calling Zac and backing out. Because this all felt so familiar, and familiarity wasn't something Sophie wanted to ever experience. Especially not with men.

Drawing a long breath, Sophie lifted her chin and told herself silently she was strong. That no matter what, Zac's opinion didn't define her. That she would go on this date and smile and enjoy herself. For her, not him. And that she wouldn't, under any circumstances, fall for him.

"It's just a fake date, no big deal," she said, aloud this time, because her hands were still clammy and her heart was picking up speed in her chest. "And he's nice. Okay, maybe not nice. But not bad. He's not bad."

Unlike him.

Sophie shook the thought away before it could bring her down. It had been so long since she allowed herself to think about the life she had left behind that when she did it often resulted in self-doubt and worry.

People talked about addicts and abusers as though they were easy to identify and their markings easy to see, but that wasn't always the case. Addiction could hide behind a church-going smile, abuse behind a gentle touch and an even gentler voice. Because some of the most harmful things in life weren't shouted or thrown, awakening your inner protector. Oh no, those types of people would never be so obvious. Instead, they crept in, step-by-step, inch after inch, until they rested comfortably in your subconscious, stealing your identity. Stealing your mind.

Let me see your progress.

Sophie tried to keep the image from seeping into her mind, but it snuck in without warning—her before a floor-length mirror, naked except for her underwear, black Sharpie lines drawn around the excess inches on her thighs and stomach. Permanent so she would be forced to see it for days and remember the work she needed to give those areas.

Closing her eyes, Sophie drew a breath, then snapped her eyes back open and stared at herself. "You are intelligent. You are kind. You are driven. You are beautiful. You are worthy." Her bottom lip shook, and she blinked back tears before they made a mess of her makeup. "And it's just a fake date."

She just needed to get in her car and drive over to pick up Zac. Because there was no way she would go out without her car, without a way to leave. That trust ship sailed long ago, and if he wanted her to do this thing, then he'd have to accept a few of her tics, and transportation was one of them.

Grabbing for a tissue, Sophie blotted the corners of her eyes, then picked up her all-natural blush brush and swiped another bit of peachy coral pink across the tops of her cheekbones and down the bridge of her nose. Okay, done.

Then she turned away from her reflection and the pain it showed her, grabbed her keys from the key hook and set off for her Mini Cooper, every step away from the mirror like a jolt of oxygen to her lungs, revitalizing both her body and her mind. She'd have to remember not to linger there so long next time.

Next time.

There would for sure be a next time and a next, every single one of them a reminder of what dates used to be like. The slow smile and gentle kiss on the cheek before he crushed her with a single whispered insult. And then she'd be forced to hold it all in while inside she felt like that little girl on the swing set, never good enough for a friend.

Well, at least with ready access to her car, if Zac pissed her off, she could toss her drink at him, say screw it, and leave. Because while she might not be one hundred percent yet, she wasn't the weak person she'd once been, the person who allowed another to treat her like a possession. She would never be that person again.

But then, a part of her suspected that she would have nothing to worry about with Zac. He'd probably never insulted anyone in his life. He had a good-boy vibe to him, something that said beneath all those smirks and tattoos lay a man who would stand tall for those he loved, who wasn't afraid of hard work, and who would hold a woman long after she'd drifted off, his eyes still on her just to watch her sleep.

"Stop thinking about Zac Littleton."

"What?"

Sophie's eyes went wide as she stared around her car. "Who's there?"

A laugh broke the silence. "Your car called me again, silly. I'm on Bluetooth or whatever."

Sophie released a breath as she found her cell, and sure enough, she'd accidentally dialed Glenda; now she was on the intercom in the car. "Crap. Sorry."

"Just be glad it wasn't Zac Littleton you called when you confessed that you couldn't stop thinking about him."

"That's not what I said."

"Um, sorry. Yes, in fact, it is what you said. And besides, what's so wrong with Zac anyway? He's hot, and he's nice."

"He's not nice."

"All right, so not nice, but something."

Sophie chewed her thumbnail. "Yeah, I know. I hate that something. I mean, I don't even know what it is or how to describe it, which makes me hate it all the more."

Glenda laughed again. "How about you forget the something for now and just have a good time tonight? See how it goes from there."

"I don't like Zac Littleton."

"Sure you don't. Have fun!" Then Glenda ended the call before Sophie could try harder to convince her friend—and herself—that she had no thoughts about Zac, certainly not likeable thoughts.

But as she drove down his long driveway, cradled by pinewoods on both sides, his cabin in the far back, the tin roof with cedar wood siding stained to perfection, she knew she was lying to herself. Because she had a lot of thoughts about Zac. Too many, in fact. And not enough of them were negative thoughts, but that ended right now.

Sophie opened her car door and threw on that sass she carried around like an iron shield, then strutted to his door—all Lorde singing "Royals"—and knocked twice, prepared to tell him to hurry up, she ain't got time to wait on a man. Then the record skipped, and instead of Zac answering the door, his daughter greeted her.

"Ms. Marsh!"

"Um, Carrie-Anne . . . hi."

The little girl, who was every bit of twelve and probably didn't view herself as little, took Sophie's hand and tugged her inside.

"I was just asking Daddy which nail polish he liked better—black, green, or purple—and he said pink." She rolled her eyes, as if Sophie would totally understand the absurdity of choosing pink as a nail color.

"What?" a deep voice called. "You're a girl. Girls like pink."

Sophie's eyes lifted to find Zac standing in the hallway dressed in a button-down shirt with the sleeves rolled to his elbows and dark jeans, his hair a spiked mess like always. The look collided with his tattoos in the sexiest of ways, and Sophie prayed that her face wasn't revealing just what she thought of Zac Littleton in a dress shirt.

"Ms. Marsh, tell him he's ridiculous. Tell him he has no idea what's in style."

Biting her lip, Sophie peered back at Zac. "You're ridiculous. And you have no style."

"Is that right?" Zac edged closer, his mild cologne clouding her senses until she was uncertain whether she could speak without drooling all over him.

Dear God, attraction shouldn't be this hard to ignore. Or at the very least, they should offer medication to counter it. She swallowed and ordered her ovaries to behave. "Apparently so. Miss Carrie-Anne here says so."

"Hey," the little girl said with a grin. "No one calls me miss."

"Well, if you call me miss, then I have to do the same."

Carrie-Anne's grin widened, and Sophie reached down, grabbed the purple polish, and passed it over. "This is perfect. It'll bring out your skin tone."

She stared at the polish and then back up at Sophie. "Do I want my skin tone to be brought out?"

"Totally."

When Sophie glanced over at Zac, she found his eyes on her and a peculiar expression on his face that said he hadn't figured her out.

But before Sophie could clue him in to the hard fact that there would be no figuring her out, because she had no intentions of allowing it, a knock sounded from the front door, followed by the doorbell, then another knock.

"Coming!" Carrie-Anne squealed before darting to the door.

"Thanks for that," Zac said.

Sophie cleared her throat and peered up at him again, steeling herself for the warmth she knew she'd find on his face. "Anytime."

"Do you mean that?"

She cocked her head in question, but before she could ask what he meant, Brady and Charlie appeared, Carrie-Anne on their heels.

"So we're painting purple today."

Sophie's eyebrows lifted. "We?"

Brady grimaced down at the polish in his hand. "She makes us let her paint our nails. She calls it practice."

Carrie-Anne winked from behind them, and Sophie grinned. "Of course. A girl's got to practice."

"Will you practice with me sometime, Ms. Marsh?"

"Um . . ." Sophie checked Zac for his reaction, but he wasn't looking at her, he was looking at Carrie-Anne. Sophie could tell by his expression that he was worried about this already—how it would affect his daughter and how she would cope once it fell apart.

"Sure thing. Just name the date."

"Yay! How about tomorrow?"

"Oh, I . . ."

"Yeah, see how you like it," Brady said as he patted Zac's shoulder and went into the kitchen. "Got any leftovers?"

"Chicken-and-rice casserole."

Brady peeked back into the family room and pointed at his niece. "You?"

She grinned. "Me. But Daddy won't let me put it in the oven by myself."

"What?" Brady said, affronted. "You're fourteen years old."

"Twelve."

He waved her off. "Same thing. And you won't let her use the oven without parental supervision."

Zac smirked at his brother. "Don't feel bad. I won't let you use my oven without parental supervision either."

"Funny."

"I thought so," Sophie said grinning, and Zac's eyes locked on hers. She had no idea why she took Zac's side, but she liked the idea of having his back, and maybe him having hers in return.

"We should go," Zac said as he cleared his throat, suddenly refusing to look at Sophie. Or his brothers, she realized.

"Right."

"Thanks for watching Carrie for me," he said to Charlie.

"Hey! What about me?"

"And for watching Brady. I know he can be a handful."

"Ha. Ha."

Zac gave Carrie-Anne a big hug that seemed to embarrass her more than anything. Then he opened the door for Sophie, who, without looking at him, said, "You know guys only open the door for women so they can check out their asses, right?"

"Yep."

"So you're admitting that's what you just did?"

He winked at her as they reached Sophie's car. "That's not what I said. I said I knew that's what guys did. I didn't say that's what I did."

"But did you?" She stared him down, daring him to argue, but he only grinned back at her, the sexy smirk in full work mode.

"Sorry, that'll have to go to the grave."

Then he stood beside her at the driver's door. Both looked at the other confused.

"What are you doing?" they simultaneously asked.

"Driving," Zac said.

"Nuh-uh. This is my car. I drive."

"I don't think so. We can take your car, but I'm the driver."

"Why?"

Zac's head twitched. "Because I'm the guy."

She pointed at him. "See that. That right there? There'll be none of that in this."

"There will be plenty of that in this, or we can call the deal off right now. I don't ride. I drive."

"So do I."

Zac took a step closer. "And a part of me appreciates that about you, but there can be only one driver in this thing, and that driver is me. So either walk your cute ass around to the passenger side, or I'm going back inside and you can sweeten the town on your own."

"This is silly."

"Yet you're still standing here. Forget that I somehow have to figure out how to squeeze into this Barbie-mobile." He shook his head. "Surely there are height restrictions for this thing."

"Are you trying to piss me off?"

"Right now? Not really, but give me time."

"I'm driving."

"Okay, so drive." He started to walk away, and Sophie stomped her foot in aggravation.

"Ugh!" Clenching her fists, she smoothed her dress to calm her temper before she went off on Zac in his front yard, Carrie-Anne mere yards away in the house, probably watching them. And she seemed like such a sweet girl, despite having a pigheaded ass as a father.

"Stop."

"What did you say?" Slowly, he spun around and crossed his arms.

"I said stop."

"And . . ."

"And you can drive your truck and I'll drive my car. Then you don't have to worry about the whole squeezing-into-my-car business."

Zac considered this, his eyes checking his truck, then her tiny Mini Cooper.

"Deal."

She released a breath.

"Didn't realize you were so nervous."

"I didn't realize you'd bail on me over something as stupid as driving."

"A man's got standards, and I refuse to lower mine. I drive. End of story."

"Your stubbornness knows no bounds."

"Ditto, Ms. Marsh. Ditto."

Zac found himself glancing in the rearview mirror over and over. He'd glance at it, catch sight of the Mini Cooper, and then look back at the road, only to start the process all over again. Which was plain stupid. What was she going to do? Bail on the date before they even arrived?

Maybe.

The disappointment he felt at the thought bothered him, and he tried to make sense of why he cared at all. But the truth was, he wanted to spend time with Sophie, wanted to slowly peel back those layers of hers to discover what lay beneath them.

Which was why going to Captain Jack's might have been a mistake. Especially when he pulled onto the gravel road that led to the restaurant that overlooked Cherokee Lake and realized every other person in town had also chosen it for their Friday night.

He wanted the town to see them out together, but he'd hoped to tread slowly and more cautiously into the roaring wave of gossip that was Crestler's Key.

After parking, Zac walked over to Sophie's car and opened the driver's door. "Hope you like fish." He tried to keep his tone light, teasing, but in truth, he was every bit as nervous as he would be if this were a real first date.

"Love it."

"Good."

"Are you ready for this?" he asked as he closed her car door and waited for her to hit the automatic lock, which made him smile a little, because there wasn't a person in Crestler's Key who'd care to steal her car. They'd far more likely try to steal his truck, but that hadn't stopped him from leaving it unlocked.

"Honestly? No," she said with a laugh. "It's been a long time since I've done this, and the last thing I need is to make an idiot of myself. Then they'll hate me even more."

"I've told you, they don't hate you."

Sophie glanced up, her look tentative in the moonlight, something like doubt hidden behind that sass of hers, before she laughed. "Yeah, well, they might if I break your heart, so you'd better keep it safe in your chest. Some tell me I'm easy to fall for." She winked, but Zac couldn't bring himself to say anything insulting in reply when the only thought going through his mind was *hell yes you are.*

Instead he stared back at her and said, "I believe it," before opening the door to the waterfront restaurant, a heavy stream of noise and chatter filling their ears. The smell of grilled steak, a Captain Jack's specialty, hit them, and Zac decided to go all out tonight with steak and lobster and offered for Sophie to do the same. Who knew if he'd piss her off and this would be their one and only date.

The restaurant was a mix of rustic woods and calming greens and blues, like something you'd find at the ocean instead of in the middle of Kentucky. But Zac liked it. It reminded him of a few of his coastal favorites, and Brantley, the owner, had fresh fish brought in every weekend, so Zac could get himself a good crab cake and catch of the day, filling his inner need to be on the water, instead of managing a farm. As usual on Friday night, a live band was setting up at the back corner.

"Heya, Zac, what are you doing here on a Friday night?" Brantley called from the bar.

Zac held his breath as every head in the place turned toward the hostess podium, their eyes on Zac, a smile there, until those same eyes drifted to Zac's left, to Sophie. Then their faces, one by one, crinkled up in confusion.

As Brantley realized what he'd done, he pushed out from behind the bar and started over, his white hair gelled into place like always, his cheeks forever red, and his belly jiggling despite his occasional workouts at the Y. Some people were built a certain way no matter what they did, like God had his creation set and refused to waver.

"Uh, Zac, Sophie Marsh is beside you." Brantley scratched his head and smiled a bit at Sophie, though he didn't actually say hello or acknowledge her beyond the pained smile.

"Yeah, thanks for letting me know, Brant. But seeing as she came with me, I kind of knew that already."

Brantley's eyes turned to saucers, and he rocked back on his heels. "Oh. Oh, right." He glanced between Zac and Sophie again, like he was trying to make sense of something overly complex. For the first time, Zac understood what it must feel like to be Sophie in Crestler's Key.

"Care to grab us a table?"

"Table? Oh, right."

And then Sophie spoke up.

"Or we could just seat ourselves." She started toward an open table, but Zac grabbed her hand to pull her back, securing her to his chest and trying to laugh it off. But there was no hiding what she'd done.

Brantley's brow furrowed as he scowled at her. "I don't know what it's like in Merryville, but here, we care about service. We don't just wave our hands and tell people to find their place. We take them to their tables with a smile and a handshake and bring garlic biscuits. I bet none of the places in Merryville bring garlic biscuits either, do they? Well, you're getting some. Like it or not."

"Brant, she didn't mean—"

"I know what she meant."

Ah, damn.

Brantley set down the laminated menus with more fervor than a simple request to seat themselves should warrant, but there it was.

"Drinks?"

"Um . . . can I have a second?" Sophie asked, her voice small now.

"Typical out-of-towner," Brantley muttered. "Fine. I'll send Trixie over to help y'all."

Zac nodded with a tight smile. "Thanks, old man." Brantley sped off, clear aggravation on his face.

"That went well."

"See, I told you. I didn't do anything but offer to seat us so he didn't have to and then ask for a second to figure out what I wanted to drink."

"I know."

"So why did he freak out? Am I wearing an offensive color or something?"

Zac tried to think of a good way to explain it. Surely, Merryville residents had their quirks, like the people of Crestler's Key. It couldn't just be them.

"Back in Merryville, did people bring by soup when you were sick?"

She cocked an eyebrow. "Um, no. Why would they?"

He tried again. "Okay, how about the hardware store. Did yours let you keep a tab until you were done with your project?"

"Our hardware store was called Lowe's."

That threw him. Zac knew Merryville was bigger than their small town, but he didn't realize they were *that* kind of town. The kind that posed as a small town but allowed all the luxuries of a city—the Walmarts and Starbucks and Lowe's.

"Right. Well, I guess that'd be the problem."

"That we had a Lowe's?"

"No, the reason you're not fitting in. You're a little too city."

She jerked back and pointed a finger at herself. "Me? Do you hear my accent?"

A grin took over Zac's face. "Oh, I hear it. But I don't think you're hearing me. We are a small town as set in its ways as an elderly couple who's been married too long to remember how to function without each other. Everybody has a tic, making the whole town sort of like a clock that runs just fine."

"So you're saying I'm messing with how well the clock turns?"

"Exactly. Glad you see the problem."

"I see it about as well as I can see through motor oil."

"What?"

"I don't know. I'm frustrated."

He smirked and glanced down at the menu.

"And everyone's staring at us."

"Which is what you wanted, remember? They like me."

"Bragger."

Trixie appeared then for their drink orders, and Zac prayed Sophie would have hers figured out or this evening was going to get real bad real fast. "Y'all ready? Hey, Zac."

"How you doing, Trixie?" Zac asked as he glanced up at the waitress, who'd graduated a year or two after him in school.

"Doing good. Finally caught that rattler in my backyard."

Sophie tensed, and Zac nearly broke into fits.

"Good to hear it. All right, I'm going to have a Sam Adams. Sophie?" He eyed her, a silent plea in his eyes to make the wait worth it.

"I'll just have a water, please, no ice and no lemon."

Dear God.

Trixie walked away muttering something that sounded a lot like "uptight" and "difficult" and other words that he prayed Sophie hadn't heard.

"What was that?" he asked once Trixie was out of earshot.

"What?"

"That drink order. Couldn't you have at least ordered a mixed drink or something?"

"I'm driving."

"Yeah, so am I."

"Well, then, you shouldn't be drinking either."

"And you shouldn't order water without the damn ice. Who does that?"

"People with sensitive teeth, that's who. If I get ice in my drink, I'll be in pain all night, and then I'll turn my anger at that pain on you. So if you want to feel that wrath, go ahead, tell Ms. Glare-A-Lot to add the ice. Make it double ice. Who needs any water in it, anyway? And while you're at it, throw in the lemon, which is certain to be nonorganic and loaded with pesticides. Which you would know because they're probably from your farm. But sure, put those chemicals in my water. Won't kill me or anything. Oh, wait. The FDA said they *will*, in fact, kill you over time. With a little thing called cancer. But by all means, give me cancer just so I don't piss off the wait staff."

"Here's your perfect, no-ice, no-lemon water."

Zac closed his eyes as Trixie set down the water, Zac's beer, and a basket of garlic biscuits.

"What are you doing here with her anyway? I thought you didn't like her like the rest of us."

"I—" Zac started, but Sophie pushed out of her chair before he could continue.

"I need a moment please." Sophie raced for the door that led outside more quickly than he'd ever seen her walk.

Zac feared he'd made a terrible decision choosing Captain Jack's for their first date. He should have chosen somewhere quieter with just a few people there so he could introduce Sophie slowly. Instead, he'd thrown her to the wolves.

"Guess she didn't like the water after all." With a laugh, Trixie disappeared back into the kitchen.

Zac followed after Sophie, wishing he would have anticipated this disaster, but apparently good sense was missing from his list of ingredients.

Pushing out the back door onto the deck that led to the dock, Zac inhaled the earthy scent of lake water mixed with the surrounding pines. For a moment he didn't see her, and he feared she'd hightailed it out of there, screw him and everyone else in this town. But as he edged down the sloping ramp to the dock, he caught sight of her standing at the end, her arms wrapped around herself, that blond-and-strawberry hair of hers blowing in the breeze off the water.

In that moment, he wanted to watch her to see what she would do next, but he knew if this was going to work, if she was going to trust him, he had to be the friend they claimed he was.

"Tough crowd, huh?" he asked. When she didn't reply, he stopped beside her, his shoulder brushing against hers, but she didn't move away. Like maybe she needed the feel of him there for support, even if she wouldn't ask for it.

"They hate me."

"They don't—"

"They do."

"Okay, maybe some of them might not be so fond of you, but you know what?"

"What?" She peered up at him for the first time, and he caught the redness in her eyes. She blinked, and a single tear slipped free and glided down her cheek. Tentatively, Zac reached up to swipe it away.

"Screw them."

Her eyes widened a bit as she glanced back at the restaurant to make sure no one had heard, and he had to laugh at her response.

"That's right, I said it. Screw them. You can only be yourself. Anything else isn't good enough. Just you being you. And if they don't like it—hell, if *anyone* doesn't like it—then screw them."

The corners of her lips twitched, and she sniffled. "I have a hard time with that sentiment."

"I can see that. Well, except when it comes to me. You seem to screw me whenever you can. Oh, wait."

She burst out laughing, and a surge of relief washed over Zac that felt an awful lot like happiness. Could making another person happy be the magic to making yourself happy? It was a peculiar thing, and certainly something he experienced every day with Carrie-Anne, but that was different. She was his daughter, and that kind of happiness existed on an entirely different level from this. Yet as he bumped Sophie's shoulder, causing her to laugh once more, he thought he could get used to this happiness thing. And the woman who had caused it.

"Want to eat or leave?"

Sophie rolled back her shoulders and lifted her head. "Nobody's stopping this woman from eating."

He grinned, and they turned back toward Captain Jack's. As they went back in, she said, "But I'm planning the next date."

"Next date, huh?"

Their gazes connected, and Zac could swear he felt a charge fill the air, a spark building between them, linking them together.

"You know, if you're game," she added.

He opened the door and felt her arm brush his chest, the charge spiking. "Name the day and I'm yours."

Zac caught the light smile on her face before following her to their table, his mind and heart full of thoughts and feelings he hadn't had in a long, long time. Now how to shut that down before the unthinkable happened and he found himself falling for his fake date.

They sat back down as Trixie made her way over, a hand on her hip as she peered down at Sophie. "Let me guess. Allergic to half the things on the menu, so you need something made special for you."

"Now, look—" Zac began, but Sophie cut him off.

That prize-winning smile of hers spread across her face. "I appreciate your concern. Maybe you're not the old wench I thought you were after all. But as it happens, I don't have any allergies. Unless you count bad manners, then yeah, I suppose I'm feeling a little allergic to you right now." She paused, her whole face transforming in barely contained glee as Trixie's mouth fell slack. "So just a cheeseburger all the way will do, thanks."

Trixie's eyes narrowed. "Fries all right?"

"Fries sound perfect, thank you." Sophie turned her sparkling gaze on Zac, begging him to react. He managed to cover his laugh with a cough.

"Um, same. Yeah," he said, bypassing the steak and lobster in the name of solidarity with his date. He closed his menu and passed it to Trixie, who glared in response, but he wasn't too worried. After all, it wasn't the first time she'd glared at him and likely wouldn't be the last. But as soon as she was out of earshot, Sophie crossed her arms, and that sass of hers turned on him.

"Why do I get the feeling I'm going to pay for that kindness of yours later?"

Zac sat back in his chair and tried not to grin. "Well, I did agree to help your image. Might as well keep up my end of the bargain. Especially since I expect you to keep up yours."

"The part where I date you. Even though you could date any woman you'd like."

"I don't want to date just 'any woman.'" He almost finished with "I want to date you," but managed to stop himself before that nugget of truth slipped free and ruined him for good. Instead, he decided it was time he infused a little real date stuff into their fake date. "Why did you move to Crestler's Key? I know the rumors, but what's the truth?"

"The rumors?"

Instead of going into the real rumors around town, the ones that said she came to steal her grandmother's home and everything the poor old woman owned, he said, "You know, that you visited the market last year, took one look at me, and knew you needed to meet me."

She laughed, the sound so light it brought a smile to his face. "So the town is saying I bought a farm just so I could meet you? Who exactly is spreading this rumor?"

Zac lifted his hands. "No idea, but I've assured them you hate me far too much for such nonsense."

"I don't hate you."

"No?"

"No."

Suddenly Zac felt his heart pick up speed. His eyes locked on this woman before him, too beautiful for her own good, yet he wasn't sure she had a clue of the impact she had on those around her. On him.

"What about you? Are the rumors about you true?"

He cracked a smile and glanced out into the restaurant. "Ah, that."

"So married once, right? Out in Texas? What did you do out in Texas?"

Besides watch his wife walk away with her doctor? He couldn't say that. For once, he wouldn't let his anger at Lora ruin his happiness. "Mainly, I coached at a local high school—football."

"I bet you loved it."

He thought back to those days, the intensity of game day, how the whole community came out on Friday nights. "I did. It's a culture out there—everything to them. It was nice being a part of something that meant so much to the town."

"So why not coach when you moved back here? What made you open Southern Dive?"

The evening crowd had filtered in, every table full now, a thousand conversations happening all around them. Yet as Zac met Sophie's stare again, it was as though they were the only ones in the room. It was unsettling in the best possible way, and he found himself leaning closer, eager to invade a bit more of her space as he revealed the truth he wouldn't have admitted to anyone else. "I guess I didn't want any part of that life to come with me here. I wanted to start over, fresh. I didn't want reminders of what I'd had—what I'd lost. Of what Carrie-Anne had lost. Does that make sense?"

"Yeah . . . it does." She blinked once, like she'd been in a trance, and Zac released the breath he'd been holding as Trixie brought over their burgers, releasing the tension of the moment.

They ate in silence for a beat before Zac realized she now knew far more about him than he knew about her. "So what's up with all the baking? It's like foreplay to men, you know. You have half the town under your spell now."

A loud laugh broke from her lips, and he grinned as he took a pull from his beer.

"Foreplay, huh? I guess it is for me, too. I love it. Nana taught me everything I know. I used to stand on this old wooden stepstool at her side and watch her create magic in the kitchen. Warm cinnamon and spice would fill the air as it baked, and I'd think, now this is heaven."

She glanced up wistfully at the ceiling and then stuck her thumb into her mouth to suck off a fallen drop of mustard from her burger. Zac suppressed the urge to groan as he watched her.

"I guess I've made some of the recipes my own over the years, but to me, baking brings me back to center. It reminds me of simpler times, when there was nothing to worry about but making sure I watched the clock so I didn't overcook the turnovers. Back then, Nana didn't have a timer, probably wouldn't have used one even if she did."

She popped another French fry into her mouth, and Zac took another long pull of his beer, then two, so he could look at her without her seeing every thought going through his mind, half of them far too indecent to be having in a restaurant full of the town and all their gossip.

Still, with her long hair cradling her perfect face, her eyes bright from her memory, he couldn't help but stare. And the surprise of it all—she was staring right back at him.

Trixie returned then with their check, breaking the connection, and Zac thought he was liking his old schoolmate less and less by the second. "Getting crowded now, so thought I'd bring this on over." She dropped the check, and Zac instantly took it, placed his credit card inside, and handed it back to her.

"You didn't have to pay," Sophie said after Trixie walked away.

"Sure I did. It was my date."

She cocked her head and grinned. "So that means you'll let me pay for our next date?"

Zac opened his mouth to say yes, whatever, none of this was real after all. But it felt real, far too real for him to allow her to pay for anything. "How about I agree to consider it?"

"The date or letting me pay?"

"A man would have to be crazy to turn down a date with you."

A smile played at her lips as they made their way outside and to their cars. A clear, starry night shone above them, the air crisp, a soft breeze causing the trees to sway, everything about the moment easy and relaxed, not at all like the rest of Zac's life. He found himself wishing they could extend the evening, even if no words passed between them, just Sophie beside him and the stars above.

"Well, this is me," she said, motioning to her car. Zac opened her door and leaned on it as she slipped around to the other side, but not inside the car just yet. Instead she faced him, the door the only thing between them. The wind blew her hair, and several loose strands flew over her face, but Zac didn't dare reach out to tuck them away from her face. Separated by just a few inches, her floral scent invading his senses, he feared that if he touched her, if his fingertips felt her hair, her skin, he would lose all control and kiss her. Already, every fiber in his body ached for him to close the small distance, to see if she tasted as sweet as her baked goods.

But before he lost the fight with himself, Sophie graced him with one more smile and said, "Good night, Zac."

"Good night, Sophie"

He closed her car door and watched her pull away.

Chapter Eight

Sophie felt the bed dip beside her and adjusted in her sleep, her hands reaching out, only to connect with something and shift away. She tried to back up, but he had pressed a firm hand to her stomach, stopping her.

"It's okay."

"What are you doing?"

He cocked his head and brushed a strand of hair from her face. She caught the look in his eyes, a look she'd seen more times than she cared to lately, and it had started to frighten her. A look like he was walking the delicate line between sanity and absolute psychopath.

He didn't speak, didn't even open his mouth. Instead he climbed on top of her, while she tried to back away, her claustrophobia rising.

Finally he whispered, "Shh, it's okay." She fought against him, but he had a foot of height on her and more than eighty pounds of muscle.

"I'm not going to hurt you. I'm helping you. Now put the blanket over your head."

"No!" She startled awake, a cold sweat breaking across her neck, and her nightgown stuck to her like she'd climbed into the shower in her sleep.

Sophie pushed her sheets off and rushed to the bathroom, lifted the toilet lid, and started to make herself vomit until she caught her reflection. Seeing the absolute fear there, she slowly closed the lid and sat back, tears filling her eyes and spilling down her cheeks before she could stop them.

It was over, she'd left, and he couldn't hurt her now. But that was part of what made him so evil—he hadn't ever hurt her. Not physically, at least. Which made getting the restraining order approved by the court a lengthy endeavor and the divorce an even lengthier one. He'd never once hit her, never even gave her a bruise.

On the outside.

The scars from his hits were layered within, over her heart and self-esteem—pink and white markings all through her mind. Evidence of just how badly he'd broken her.

And she'd never seen it coming.

A Xanax cocktail later, Sophie was all smiles as she walked toward the fire station entrance, a basket full of fresh pastries in hand to bribe them through their bellies.

The fire department's annual bachelor auction to raise money for the fire station was just two months away, and every person who attended the auction would receive a basket of fruit and a plant to celebrate summer. Apparently, everyone in town attended, and Littleton Farms always provided the baskets. But this year, Sophie intended for Fresh Foods to supply those baskets and plants.

Several of the firefighters were washing one of their giant red trucks when she approached. "Hi there," she said, then lifted up the basket so the vanilla and cinnamon and spice smells would float over to them. "Y'all hungry?"

Immediately the men stopped what they were doing to get a peek at what she'd brought.

"I was looking for Justin. Is he around?"

"Right here. What can I do for you?"

Sophie turned to see a man standing just inside the brick fire station. His eyes squinted as he peered at her like he already didn't trust her and wanted to check out the situation before he fully committed.

"Hey there. Well, I brought these treats by in hopes of having a little talk with you about the bachelor auction."

"Yeah? What about it?"

"Well, rumor has it you give out fruit baskets and plants to all the attendees. I'd like to offer for Fresh Foods to supply those this year."

"We get them from Littleton Farms."

Unwrapping the basket, Sophie passed out the lemon tarts and turnovers to the firefighters before stepping up to Justin and motioning to the basket.

"Apple or cherry?"

He fidgeted, his eyes on the perfectly glazed, flaky crusts. Nana had taught Sophie how to make the perfect turnovers every time by using shortening instead of butter, and ever since, she'd never met a person who could refuse them. She held out a turnover, wrapped prettily in Fresh Foods paper wrapping, then secured with a sticker boasting the Fresh Foods daisy and butterfly logo.

"Miss, I get that you're just trying to find your ground here, but Zac is an old friend of mine."

Sophie almost rolled her eyes. Every single person in this town was an old friend of Zac's. She'd like to meet a person who didn't consider him or herself a friend of Zac's. Didn't the man have any enemies? But instead of saying as much, she bit her tongue and flashed him another bright smile. "Right. You used to play football together, right?"

Justin glanced from the basket to her. "Who told you that?"

"Zac. He's the one who sent me here to talk to you about the auction." Which wasn't exactly true, but it would be after she called Zac and ordered him to vouch for her story.

"Oh. All right then."

"And I know y'all like to do fruit and all, but I'd be happy to give you a deal on pastry baskets as well and even jelly and jams for the event if you're interested."

Justin didn't look convinced. "And Zac told you to stop by?"

Sophie waved her hand in the air. "Yep. We're great friends. Hang out all the time."

His eyebrows lifted. "You and Zac."

"Mmm hmm." Sophie couldn't bring herself to tell another lie and was already feeling the weight of this one on her back. She was anxious to leave so she could call Zac and turn the lie into some truth.

"Well, all right then," Justin repeated. "I guess if Zac is okay with it . . ."

"He is. Totally is."

"Okay. I guess, then, why don't you pull together some numbers for me?"

Sophie fought the urge to jump up and down and punch the air. "Of course," she said, her voice as even as a spray tan. "About a hundred baskets?"

"More like five hundred or so this year. We're teaming up with a few neighboring towns to make it a collective event."

"Wow." Sophie covered her excitement by walking away to place the basket on a bench; the remaining firefighters rushed over and emptied it almost immediately. "Okay, then." She laughed, then waved to Justin. "See you later. And I'll get those numbers to you by tomorrow morning."

"Sounds good. And maybe bring by some more of these when you come?" He lifted up a half-eaten cherry turnover. "You know, if it's not too much trouble?"

She tilted her head and offered a true Southern-lady smile. "Absolutely. You take care now." She waved good-bye, then slipped into her car and dialed Zac even before she'd pulled out of the station, her left wedge sandal tapping away in impatience.

"Come on! I know you're around. Pick up already."

"I did."

"Oh! Sorry about that."

"Is there something I can do for you, Ms. Marsh, or were you calling to hear the sound of my voice?"

Maybe a little of that, but Sophie refused to admit it to him. "Actually, Mr. Thinks One Date Equals A Girl Gone Wild For You, I need a favor."

"Does it involve accepting your apology for that insult? Because I think that'll take a bit. You know, like another date. Your pick this time, remember?"

A smile crept across her face. "I remember. And I'm thinking on it. But for now, I need to know something."

"Which is?"

Sophie turned right and headed toward Fresh Foods the long way, which might or might not require her to drive by Littleton Farms, where she might or might not hope to spy a certain tattooed farmer. "What's your stance on lying?"

Chapter Nine

"Lying? Like in a bed with you beside me? Because I could get behind that idea. Or are we talking the slap-on-the-wrist kind?"

Zac tucked his phone under his chin and picked up his jeans, slipping them on as he tried to continue the conversation without dropping his cell and losing the call. Which was about as crazy as hell, because he could call her right back, but then what if she didn't answer?

And he'd officially become *that* dude.

"The pray-to-God-for-forgiveness kind. What are you doing anyway? It sounds like you keep covering the receiver."

Zac placed his phone in his mouth and tugged on a Littleton Farms T-shirt, then returned the phone to his ear. "Getting dressed. What about you?"

"It's nine, though."

"Yeah."

"I'd think you'd be up earlier."

"Had a late night."

He smiled at the pause on the other end, the sharp inhale. Maybe he wasn't the only one having reactions around here.

"Oh."

"Carrie had a last-minute school project. Took me all night to finish it."

The relieved breath he heard sent a surge straight to his chest. Zac ordered himself to slow down, keep this in check, or he'd never be able to control his feelings. It had already become a struggle. The way he looked for her in town, the way his ears pricked to listen when he heard someone say her name. It'd been less than a week since their date, four days to be exact, and he was going out of his mind to see her again. Which wasn't healthy for a man like him who had responsibilities and obligations and other shit that meant he didn't have time for anything or anyone else.

"Sounds like you're in need of some rest."

"Why, you offering to help me get some?"

"You are such a ridiculous flirt."

"I told you, only with you."

The phone went silent again, and Zac leaned against his dresser, his arms crossed. "What do you need me to lie about? I should warn you that I lie about as good as I apply nail polish, and Carrie will be the first to tell you that's a nightmare. So ask at your own risk. I may out you without realizing it."

"I told Justin Zilla at the fire station that you sent me there to talk about supplying the baskets at the bachelor auction this year."

"And why would I do that?"

Another pause and he could almost see her chewing that thumbnail of hers, that guilty spark in her eyes. "You know, because you want me to have their business this year."

At that, Zac burst into laughter. "Want you to have it? I agreed to help you impress the town, not hand over half the farm's earnings."

"I know, I know. But please. This will be huge for us, and maybe we could split it because they're doing a new auction this year that includes some neighboring towns. Instead of the normal one hundred baskets, he needs five hundred. So maybe we split it, which is still way more than you normally do."

A knock on the door interrupted Zac's thoughts, and he opened it to find his daughter on the other side, tapping her watch and her foot in time. "We need to go or we'll be late," she whispered.

"Give me a second."

"A second to think about it or a second to call Justin and confirm my story, because I know he's going to ask you. Nobody in this town can do a thing without calling everybody else to make sure it happened."

Zac grinned at the phone. "Actually, I was talking to Carrie-Anne."

"Sorry. I'm a little tense."

"And why's that?"

"Well, the lying thing. It makes me jittery. I need you to hurry up and agree, or I'm going to need another Xanax to calm myself down."

Another Xanax? Zac filed that away in his mind as something to uncover later. Tons of people took stuff for all sorts of reasons, so he wasn't about to judge. But he was curious.

"Now we don't want that. Let me make sure I understand this—you want me to lie to make your lie truthful?"

"Exactly!" She exhaled. "It's so nice to talk to someone who gets what I'm saying. So, you'll do it?"

To anyone else, Zac would tell them they got themselves into this mess and they could get themselves out. Then he'd smile and say he'd be sure to say a prayer to help it along. But somehow, instead of telling Sophie to figure it out on her own, he found himself smiling like an idiot, smitten by this woman who drove him insane ninety percent of the time.

"All right. I'll cover you, but you have to do something for me."

"I'm listening."

"Our next date. This Friday."

"If I didn't know any better, I'd suspect you were growing fond of me."

"Now let's not get carried away. I just need to keep up appearances here."

"Right . . . appearances."

"So, Friday then?"

"Actually, no, Saturday. I've been trying to go to all the local organic farms who have U-Picks to check out their layout, so I'm visiting one in Tennessee on Saturday. Just over the border. You game?"

"First lying, now spying on the competition? You trying to turn God against me or something?"

Sophie laughed, and the sound filled him with such contentment that he almost asked her to do it again. "Not possible, Zac Littleton. Your name has been on God's good list since you were born. But no harm in a girl tempting you to the dark side from time to time. Test out those golden morals and all."

"Ah . . . so you're a temptress now?" His voice went low as he asked it, new thoughts circling through his mind, each more dangerous than the last. Sophie in his bed, him over her, that spark and sass of hers taking the ordinary to the extraordinary. And damn it, now he was hard.

"If it works. Did it work?" she asked, her tone dropping to match his, a hint of sultry in the sweet.

"I'd say so. See you Saturday."

"Are you hanging up?"

"Yeah. Apparently I have to call Justin Zilla and dish that white lie of yours. Let's hope I deliver it better over the phone than I would in person or you're screwed."

"Screwed, huh?"

Ah hell, there it was again.

"See you soon, Zac."

"Later." He hung up and walked into his bathroom to help himself calm down, then set out into the hallway.

"You're smiling," Carrie said.

He wrapped an arm around his daughter. "So I am, kiddo. So I am."

The long, winding drive into Hamilton Stables always made Zac feel like he was entering another world. Lush green pastures, white fencing that rivaled the snow's brilliance, a staff dressed in shirts and hats embroidered with the Hamilton Stables logo, the pride both on their clothes and across their faces. These people lived and breathed this farm, and while Zac knew farming could break a spirit as much as it could emblazon it, he'd never once seen anyone on the Hamilton Stables staff appear anything but thankful to be here.

It made Zac wish he could re-create the same sense of joy at Littleton, but he suspected happiness like what was found here had less to do with management and more to do with some magical dirt that possessed anyone who stepped foot on it.

Or maybe he was just an ass, and that was why his staff didn't wear a grin all the damn time. But it did make him wonder how Sophie's staff acted. Were they all giggles and smiles like Hamilton Stables's staff, or did they work with their heads down like his staff?

"Daddy?"

"Huh?" Zac peered over at his daughter.

"You parked. We're here."

"Right. Sorry." He opened his door and closed it quickly, eager to get his thoughts right again. This organic farmer he was pretending to date had loosened a bolt or two in his brain, and he kept drifting off into regions he had no right to explore.

"Late. Again."

Zac glanced up at the same time that Carrie-Anne squealed, "Aunt Kate," and took off running toward his sister.

"I told him to hurry up, but he was on the phone with Ms. Marsh again, and he never gets off when she calls. It's ridiculous."

"Hey, it doesn't count as late if we didn't set a time," Zac said, hugging Kate close.

But Kate pushed him playfully, her long red ponytail swinging with the move, her green eyes flashing. "We did have a time, loser."

"Well, then, I must have forgotten." He winked and then dodged out of Kate's grasp before she could push him again.

"Emery has important things to do. You should respect her time."

"Like what?" He stared at his sister.

"Um. Like . . ."

"I'm listening."

"All right, fine, she's here all day, but that's not the point."

"Aunt Kate, can I go on down to see him?"

"You go ahead, honey." Kate grinned at her niece, and Zac thought he really shouldn't give Kate such a hard time. But then he realized that if he didn't, no one would, and everybody needed someone to keep them in line.

Kate waited until Carrie-Anne cleared the barn, well on her way to the practice ring behind it, to turn on her brother. Zac wished he'd dropped Carrie off and left before Kate had an opportunity to question him.

Already talk of Zac and Sophie together at Captain Jack's had spread around town, which meant Kate knew and would want to know why someone else had to tell her that her brother was dating someone.

"So, what's the deal with Sophie Marsh, and why did I have to hear about it from Patty instead of you?" And there it was.

"I don't recall you calling me every time you went out with someone when you were dating."

Kate crossed her arms. "Different. I have three brothers, each of you ready to throw a punch at any guy who even thought about talking to me. I had to keep my dates a secret to protect them. You're doing it to be secretive. The question is why?"

"I'm not being secretive. We went out. It's not really a big deal."

Kate released a sarcastic laugh, and Zac glanced past her to Carrie-Anne getting set up on her favorite horse, Barkley, for her weekly riding lesson with Emery, who was married to Trip Hamilton, the eldest of the Hamilton brothers. It seemed like yesterday that Emery and Kate were running around the farm, Emery always a tiny thing, but she was born to be a rider. Still, no one expected her to go on to become a successful jockey and now jockey trainer.

"Are you going to answer me?"

He was still watching his daughter, and the thought of her suffering a fall like Emery had suffered in the Kentucky Oaks was enough to make him question whether he should allow her to ride at all. But Carrie-Anne had put her hands on her hips and told him if she was allowed to go diving, then she should be allowed to ride a horse. And that ended the argument right there because she was right.

"Zac. Are you going to answer me?"

"Wasn't planning to."

"Seriously? You're dating a woman. This warrants a conversation. I mean, I thought you hated Sophie. Sure, she's cute in that polished-for-a-TV-movie kind of way, but she has to grate on your nerves. That smile? Come on."

He stared at his sister, his patience growing thinner by the second. "What's wrong with her smile?"

"Nothing, but she sure throws it around a lot. Seems odd, right? I don't know if you can trust a person who smiles that much. Gotta have skeletons in her closet right, and—wait a second."

Zac glanced over to find her pointing at him. "Oh. My. God. You like her."

"What?"

"Don't even try to deny it. I can see it all over your face. You're fighting to stay quiet, but you want to defend her. You *are* defending her."

"So what if I defend her? You're pissing all over her because she smiles too much? Who does that? Since when is smiling a problem? I like it."

Kate clapped her hands together and grinned. "Oh my God."

"You said that already."

"*You* are *totally* smitten!"

"Shut up."

And now she was laughing. Loudly. Loud enough that Trip and

Alex came out of the barn, where Zac hadn't even known they'd been working, to see what all the fuss was about.

"What did we miss?" Alex asked as he wrapped an arm around Kate and kissed his wife on the cheek, then lifted her hand to his face and kissed her palm, as if one show of affection wasn't enough.

"Zac likes a girl."

He rolled his eyes and stepped back. "Freaking hell, what are you, fifteen?"

"Hey, I'm not the one with a schoolyard crush."

"All right, that's my cue." Zac started for the backseat of his truck to get Carrie's bags, and Kate continued her jokes.

"Does she know you like her? Does she like you back? Or did she ditch you after she realized that you talk in your sleep?"

"I don't . . ." Zac trailed off and shook his head, stopping himself from letting his sister bait him. "This conversation is over."

"Do you want me to put in a good word for you? Tell her you can cook real good or something? Or wait, she's a baker, right? So that won't impress her. I've got it!" She snapped her fingers, and Zac contemplated leaving without saying good-bye to Carrie just so he could escape the scrutiny. "You need to fix something. Maybe her car or something at her house. You're, like, weirdly handy, and girls totally love that."

He stared at his sister. "Are you seriously trying to give me dating advice when you ended up with this one?" He nodded toward Alex, who simply laughed good-naturedly.

"Well, he's got you there, Red."

"He just insulted you."

"Hey, if the shoe fits," Trip said, knocking knuckles with Zac. "Want a beer? Save you from this conversation?"

"Appreciate it, but I'm heading into town for a few errands."

"All right, suit yourself."

"Why aren't you offering me a beer?" Alex called after Trip as they disappeared back inside the barn.

Kate remained behind. "Hey."

Zac glanced up. "Hey."

"I'm just messing with you."

"I know." He flashed her a grin to let her know he wasn't angry. "I grew up with you, remember? I'm well versed in your antics."

"But seriously, though. If you like her as much as I think you do, then don't let your fears keep you from going for it. Maybe all those smiles will rub off on you a little. You could use a bit of that happiness."

He shrugged. "I don't know. It's early. We'll see how it goes." Then he called out a good-bye to Carrie-Anne because he knew she wouldn't want him to come over and kiss her cheek or hug her in front of the other two girls who took lessons with Emery. He waved good-bye to the others before disappearing back into his truck where he could think without anyone around to judge or mock him.

Zac hadn't told anyone about his and Sophie's agreement, partially because he knew his family would make fun of him, but also because he was starting to question his motives for asking Sophie, of all women, to fake the dating thing. He'd spent one evening with Ms. Organic, and every evening since, he'd contemplated how he could repeat the date without coming on too strong. His thoughts drifted to her and that sweet, yet full-bodied laugh of hers, and how within it he would catch glimpses of a sadness that made him wonder what had happened to cause it. And why she couldn't let it go.

In short, he wanted to know more about her—everything about her—and that scared the ever-loving shit out of him. Because what if this was all for her reputation with the town, nothing more. Or worse, what if she decided to give it a go, like him, only to leave once he'd handed over his heart?

His thoughts drifted back to the morning Lora left. He had woken to find her sitting at the edge of the bed beside him, a bag in her hand. He'd discovered the affair the day before and was stupid enough to believe that she felt bad about it, that he had the upper hand. But he realized in that moment that he had been a fool. She never intended to stay.

So he got up and all but dragged her to Carrie's room and asked her to look at her daughter. Then he asked her how a person of any heart at all could leave such a perfect little girl. His feelings be damned—he didn't want that for Carrie.

Lora started crying and said she couldn't be a good mom to Carrie, not like she deserved, that it would be better to have no mom than her. She started for the door at the very moment that Carrie awoke, calling for her.

He would never forget the way his sweet daughter ran after her mother, crying for her to come back, her bare feet covered in grass clippings as she watched Lora drive off without a backward glance.

It took everything in Zac not to shout obscenities at his wife, but that wouldn't help his little girl through the pain. So instead, he squatted down beside her and pulled her into his lap, where he would let her cry against his chest for another hour. His body was coiled so tightly from the effort not to join Carrie in the tears that he wasn't sure he'd be able to stand once her tears had dried.

Finally, Carrie, not five years old, had looked up at him, her eyes bloodshot, her cheeks soaked. With her bottom lip trembling, she asked if he was leaving her, too. And that was when Zac lost it. Right there, a grown man on his knees before his little girl. He assured her that he would never leave her. He would die first. He would never put anyone or anything above her; she could count on him. He promised her again and again until her tiny eyes appeared less afraid and more . . . heartbroken.

But that would heal over time. Zac had spent every day since making sure Carrie knew she was loved, knew she might not have a mother, but she had a family—a father, grandparents, aunts, and cousins—and friends who all loved her. People who would never leave her.

It had taken a solid year for her to smile like she meant it, but finally the little girl he knew came back to him, a notch of heartbreak on her heart. But it made her stronger, and instead of her heart turning hard, like his, she became the most loving child he could imagine. Never turning away a friend, never killing a bug, forever saving anything and anyone she could—loving despite her circumstance. And in truth, Zac felt he could learn a lot from his daughter.

Though a man's heart wasn't so easily mended.

Gripping the steering wheel now, Zac veered right onto the main stretch of road that took him from Triple Run back to Crestler's Key, where he would throw himself into Southern Dive for the next several hours. Maybe then he could forget what had brought him back home and instead remember that maybe things like this were a blessing in disguise. They were happy here. Mostly.

After parking behind the shop, he went inside, not surprised to find Charlie there. Charlie had been running the place while Brady handled dive lessons and Zac handled things at the farm. It was tough to keep it all going, but with the three of them, they made it work.

"Hey," Charlie said, "thought you were visiting Kate."

"I did. Dropping Carrie there to stay the night tonight."

Charlie's eyes lifted. "What's that tone?"

"Nothing." Zac tossed his keys onto the counter and went behind it to check the dive lesson schedule for the next few weeks.

"Doesn't sound like nothing. You sound pissed."

"I am."

"Is this about Kate giving you a hard time at the farm?"

He spun around. "She called you."

"She might have."

"Perfect. Absolutely perfect."

Charlie set down the stack of magazines in his hand and turned toward his brother. "What's the big deal?"

"You mean besides the whole damn family thinking I've got a thing for Sophie Marsh? Nothing. No big deal at all."

"And you don't have a thing for Sophie Marsh?"

"Of course not."

Charlie went back to filling the magazine rack. "Right."

"You got something to say? Say it."

"All right, fine. You can think whatever you want, deny it as long as you like, but that doesn't change the fact that we know you. And we know when someone's affecting you. Sophie Marsh is. Call it what you like—hate, love, *lust*, whatever the hell you want. But you feel something for that woman, and you might as well explore it. Death's coming for us all, man. Might as well give life the attention it deserves while we can."

Zac leaned against the counter and stared out over the shop. "It's not about that."

"Then what?"

"It's . . ." He ran both hands over his face and sighed. "I don't know. I just don't want to screw things up."

"With Sophie?"

"No. With Carrie. She's happy now, ya know? I don't want to invite anyone into our world just to have that person leave her again."

"And you think Sophie would leave?"

Zac shrugged. "I don't know. We're not anything—not even friends, really—so I can't say what goes on in her head. But I get the feeling she's a breath away from running. Like there's something else behind that smile, and the tiniest push could have her packing up."

"She bought the farm, spent a fortune revitalizing it, and then created the Fresh Foods brand. I don't think she's going anywhere. And nobody said you've got to be talking about forever. Carrie's older now, she gets that you need to date. Hell, she's the one who asked you to do it."

"Yeah, maybe."

"So just go slow. We're not talking marriage here. Just get to know her a little. See if there's even anything there between you."

Zac already knew there was something between them. They had the sort of chemistry people dreamed about, but chemistry was only one piece of this thing. The problem was Zac didn't have the time or energy to start something, only to have it end painfully for everyone involved.

"I don't know."

"Just think about it."

He grabbed his keys and started for the door.

"Where you going?"

"Home."

"But you just got here."

Zac stopped at the door, the guilt at leaving someone hanging always there, reminding him that the days were never long enough to get everything done, to help everyone who needed his help. He brushed his hair out of his face. He was tired, dawn-of-the-dead tired, but he shouldn't leave Charlie to do everything. "Need help?"

Charlie opened his mouth, but then took in his brother and closed it. "What time did you start at the farm this morning?"

"Four."

"Nah, go home. I'm almost done anyway. I'll close up."

"You sure?"

"Yeah, but hey. Brooks called me, said he tried you, but didn't get you. He'll be in town for a few days. Wants to meet up."

"Wow, thought he ditched town for good."

Brooks was one of Zac's best friends growing up and, to Zac's knowledge, the only person besides him to move away. Of course, Zac came back, but Brooks owned an investment company now and produced money like most people breathed air.

"He said he had some business in Lexington and planned to drive down to visit his parents' graves. Asked about getting drinks, and I said sure. You can back out if you need to."

"Nah, it'll be good to catch up."

"All right, then. I'll text him back that we're game and let Brady know."

"Sounds good." Zac nodded a thanks and then set out for home, eager to shower off the day and lose himself in a project. Or maybe he'd let himself pass out early so he could recover before starting all over again tomorrow.

He thought of his organic farming enemy then, curious if she might be home, too. Then he decided that maybe instead of spending the evening on some project that didn't really matter, he'd grab a beer and sit out on his front porch.

And then he'd call Sophie Marsh.

Chapter Ten

Sophie signed her name at the check-in at Magnolia's Nursing Home, smiled a hello to the attendant, then walked to the common room where they'd brought Nana for her visit today. A slight floral scent mixed with a chemical cleaning-type smell hung in the air, and Sophie's heart pinched in guilt at the thought of Nana smelling the weird scent all day when she was a born baker and should smell fresh bread baking all day.

The common room was crowded today. Several families were visiting, some laughing, others close to tears, and Sophie wondered which emotion would find her today.

"She's by the windows." A warm hand wrapped around Sophie's arm and squeezed. "How are you, honey?"

Sophie peered over at Melinda, Nana's favorite nurse, and smiled before offering the woman a hug. "How is she today?"

Melinda shrugged. "It's hard to say. She seemed okay when I brought her in, but you know that can switch quickly."

Sophie did. She'd been talking to Nana a few weeks ago when Nana jumped up and backed away from her granddaughter, convinced that Sophie was there to hurt her. It had taken everything in her not to cry right there; instead, she told Nana she loved her and walked away while the old woman screamed and fought against the staff, before no doubt getting an injection to calm her down.

"I don't want to upset her."

"You let us worry about that. Go get you some Nana love, sweetie. I know you miss her."

She did. Deep in her bones, she missed her. Nana was the only person in her life beyond her daddy to really love her, and missing out on that kind of love made Sophie feel like a piece of her heart had disappeared, never to turn up again.

"Go on now."

With another smile, Sophie took her time walking off to the windows that overlooked Magnolia's courtyard and gardens. From the windows, the outside world looked like something out of a fantasy, all bright reds and pinks and oranges and yellows. Beautiful in every way. Sophie understood why Nana chose to sit near the windows. She would do the same if she lived here.

Taking a seat beside her, Sophie peered over at her grandmother, whose white hair was now cut in a choppy bob, her face blessed with far too many wrinkles, her hands knobby from arthritis. But when she glanced over and those crystal blue eyes of hers hit Sophie, Nana smiled.

"Hi there."

"Hello. Is it okay if I sit with you for a while?"

"Help yourself, honey. They say it's a free country, though I have my doubts."

Sophie laughed, the moment easy, until Nana asked, "What's your name, dear?"

It wasn't the first time Nana had asked her the question, but it cut straight to her heart all the same. Like always, she grinned at her grandmother. "Sophie."

"I'm Gwendolyn. It's nice to meet you."

"Nice to meet you, too. You have quite a beautiful view here."

She nodded. "It's my favorite. Looks like a fantasy."

Sophie smiled at her words, so similar to her own thoughts on the garden. "Yes, it does."

For the next hour, they talked as strangers. Nana told Sophie about her time as a nurse during Vietnam, while Sophie talked about Fresh Foods and her hopes for where it would be in five years. Finally, Sophie knew she'd reached the end of her luck and didn't want to chance an episode. So she stood.

"Thank you, Ms. Gwendolyn. This has been a lovely afternoon."

"Thank you, child."

Sophie started for the door, then paused. "Would it be okay if I hugged you?"

Her grandmother stared quizzically at her, before her face lit.

"We're in the South, honey. No need to ask for a hug. We give them freely." Then she stood and wrapped her arms around Sophie.

It took everything Sophie had not to squeeze tightly, to beg Nana to come back to her. But she knew this hour had been a tiny gift from God, and she had no intentions of taking it for granted. So she pulled back and smiled once more. "You have a nice night. Maybe I'll see you next time."

Then she walked out of the nursing home, her heart full.

Back at her house, Sophie put her iPhone on the docking station in her kitchen, turned up Carrie Underwood, and set her eyes on her kitchen cabinets. Her visit with Nana had inspired her, and she intended to put that inspiration to good use.

For two months now, her cabinets had been half-painted, half-not. At first, she claimed she needed more chalk paint. Then paintbrushes. Then some of that fancy dark and light wax that a project like this required to make it all look right and set or whatever the wax did. But enough was enough.

The inspiration to take her old oak cabinets to a pretty seafoam color with dark wax to give them that aged look had come to her while watching an episode of *Fixer Upper*. Though, to be honest, several of her projects were the result of her obsession with the show: the crate coffee table and end tables; the old stained wagon wheel to go over her bed in her master bedroom; the mason jars turned into candleholders for her table's centerpiece.

There were more ideas than time in the day. Which led to Sophie's great problem with renovating—she liked to start a project. But finishing? Well, that was an entirely different topic. But that ended today . . . at least for the cabinets

She couldn't have guests over to her house without having to explain that she was renovating her kitchen. Of course, her only real guest was Glenda, and Glenda already knew the story and how Sophie struggled to finish a project, but still. Other people could come over. People like Annie-Jean or Patty or . . . Zac.

Just the thought sent a spiral of hope, followed quickly by dread that she couldn't shake. Why did this have to be so hard? Was she really that bruised and broken that she couldn't try to like a man? He didn't even need to know that she liked him. It would be her little secret.

The problem was that the issue wasn't him—it was her.

Sighing, she worked on a pair of latex gloves and started for the left half of her cabinets, the right already painted and pretty, facing the left all high and mighty. All judge-y. Well, it was time the left get a piece of the pretty cake. And now she was talking about her cabinets like they were people. Again.

Needing some liquid relaxation so she could turn off her brain and get to work, she poured herself a tall glass of pinot grigio, the only wine she liked. She took a sip, then two, set down her "Women Rule the World One Glass at a Time" wine glass, and started for the cabinet closest to her just as her wall phone rang.

Glaring at it, Sophie contemplated letting it go, but what if it was someone needing an order for the next day? As if that ever happened. *Just ignore it.* But even as she tapped her paintbrush against her countertop, her eyes landed on the ringing phone, and she all but ran to get it, fearful she'd miss the call and they'd think she was a snob and decide to add that to the laundry list of reasons why they shouldn't do business with her. Well, that wasn't going to happen.

"Hello?" Sophie asked, a smile on her face so it'd show in her voice. There was silence on the other end, and Sophie thought whoever it was had already hung up, until she caught what sounded like metal scraping against metal, the sound so faint she wasn't sure she'd heard it at all. Then she heard a crackling sound, followed by the dial tone.

"Well, okay, then," she said. "I didn't want to talk to you anyway."

She hung up, went back to her cabinets, and dipped her brush into the chalk paint. She started on the face of a cabinet just as she'd seen in a YouTube video on Pinterest. Soon she found herself in a pattern, coating inch after inch, until she'd finished the side she was working on.

Sophie put the brush down to pour another glass of wine when her phone rang again. With a huff, she set down her glass and checked her watch. "Ten thirty? Seriously? This had better be a mega order. Like thousands upon thousands."

"Hello?" She tapped her foot, waiting on the reply, but once again she was met with silence. "Glenda, if that's you, speak up. I'm busy finishing a project here." But then she remembered that Glenda had driven out to see her parents in Lexington and wouldn't be back until Sunday. So who then? A wrong number? Yes. Had to be.

She hung up the phone and shook out her hands, but she couldn't keep the shiver from crawling down her back, that tiny, scared voice in the back of her mind still ever present, whispering like a ghost that refused to find a grave.

Night had set in long ago, but with the storm joining it, the outside looked less dark navy and more forever black. The trees surrounding her house hid the other homes around hers from view, and the wind from the storm whistled against the windows, creating an atmosphere straight out of a horror movie.

A rumble of thunder boomed, causing the windows to rattle at the same time the phone rang again. Sophie jumped a foot in the air, her heart in her throat, before her eyes narrowed in on the damn phone. She jerked it off the receiver and pressed it to her ear.

"Now you look. I'm knee deep in chalk paint that I have next to no idea how to use. There's a storm blaring away outside like a teething baby, and you keep calling here and hanging up. So either get to the slasher part and do me in, or stop freaking calling me because this lady has had enough!"

"Slasher part?"

Oh my God. Not him. Anyone but him.

"Do you in, huh?" Zac asked, his tone entirely too playful for the horror and embarrassment of the moment.

"It's a turn of phrase."

"It's a phrase used by the insane, and not the legit kind either. What's going on?"

Sophie cringed and threw her free hand into the air, then silently stomped up and down because the last thing she wanted to do was admit to Mr. Sarcastic that she was scared. But there it was on the tip on her tongue, threatening to spill all over her carefully crafted image.

"You know I can't actually hear you saying stuff in your mind, right? You need to speak."

"I know that, smarty pants. I'm just thinking of what to say."

"Meaning you're thinking up what to say."

She chewed her thumbnail.

"How about you just go with the truth? It's easier. Plus, I'm almost to your house now, so I'll probably read it on your face even if you refuse to say it."

"What?"

"I said I'm—"

"I heard what you said! I want to know why you're doing it."

"Well, when you call someone and they answer talking about slashers, one can only assume said person is completely freaked out. Which likely is for no reason, but I couldn't live with myself if you became a victim. So I'm on my way. Almost there now."

"You can't come over here."

"Why not?"

Sophie spun around in her kitchen to peek at her family room, then her breakfast nook/dining room, because her open floor plan didn't include one of each. Her house was small even by small's standard, but worse, it was barely lived in.

Her projects were scattered here and there, some half finished, others stacked together but never actually started. And then there was the rest of the house—boxes that had never been emptied, walls that had never been painted. It looked as though she planned to move away any second. Which was why she'd decided to paint her kitchen cabinets in the first place. Glenda always gave her a hard time about her bare white walls and boring furnishings, so Sophie flipped on *Fixer Upper* and sat on her coffee table and watched back-to-back episodes until she decided it was time she made her house a home.

That was six months ago, and now if she could just dedicate a few hours to each project, she would have the home she craved. But then work liked to get in the way, and there was that one week when she came down with the flu, and then that time—

Knock, knock, knock.

Sophie jumped. "Crap."

"You know I can hear you through the phone and the door."

"Right. I just need to . . ." Sophie hung up the phone, then set it down on the kitchen counter and began racing around the house, picking up old magazines and shoes left by the door. The crochet project strewn across her breakfast table because she'd planned to make a keepsake for Glenda's sister who'd had a baby . . . three months ago. But she felt sure she'd get it to her soon. Surely before the baby graduated high school.

"Sophie, I can hear you in there."

"Coming."

"What are you doing?"

"What do you think? Cleaning up."

"I don't care if the place is dirty."

"I'm not cleaning the dirt. I'm cleaning the evidence."

"Evidence of what?"

Of how epically I fail at adulting.

Sophie thrust the pile of stuff in her hand into the coat closet, which had never once held a single coat. Then she reached for her front door's doorknob, only to realize she was still wearing the gloves from painting. She yanked them off and shoved them into the closet with everything else. Finally she opened the door, a tad breathless and completely on edge, and there he stood—all T-shirt and cargo shorts, his hair a perfect mess, his skin freshly tanned from being out on the farm.

"God, you are beautiful."

Wait, what? That was so *not her speaking.* How many times had Sophie refilled her wine glass?

"Um, what I meant to say was . . ." But there was no stopping the smile from splitting his face or him from easing past her and into her home.

"Right back at you, Marsh. How much have you had to drink?"

She held up one finger and squinted in thought. "Just the one glass."

"Refilled how many times?"

She paused. "Um . . . more than once? But I'm not drunk. I'm just a little . . ." Buzzed—120 percent buzzed. And apparently unable to filter her thoughts. She needed to rein that in while Zac was here, or things were going to get awkward fast. Especially if she started talking about his tattoos and muscles, which she couldn't seem to stop staring at.

Dear God . . .

"What are you doing here?"

"You said a slasher was calling you."

And now her embarrassment went from her head to her toes. She tried to laugh it off. "Right. See, about that—"

But just as she started to explain that she'd watched that Netflix *Making a Murderer* show last night and felt sure it had invaded her subconscious and made her worry about other things, because it couldn't be other things—couldn't—her phone rang again.

"See," she said, flinging her hand at the phone on the counter as evidence. "I told you. They won't stop calling me, and you know I'm not popular enough around here for so many phone calls."

"Okay, calm down. I'm sure it's just a telemarketer who's too scared to speak up or something. Let me answer it."

Zac walked over and picked up the phone. He waited a beat and then said, "Hello?"

He held the phone out. "Hang up."

"That's the third one."

Zac wasn't admitting that he believed her, but she could tell by the way his eyes drifted to the kitchen windows, then the family room windows, that he found it peculiar.

"Ever have these calls before?"

Sophie's thoughts drifted back to six months earlier, to the constant feeling that he was watching her, always a breath away from appearing in her path. "No."

"Well, let me do a perimeter check just to be safe."

"A what? No. It's dark out, and there's this possum that likes to come out and bark at me when I go outside too late."

Now Zac pivoted around to face her, his arms crossed as that smile of his revealed two dimples. "Possum? So first a serial killer who likes to prank call, now a man-eating possum. Don't know who you pissed off in the universe, Marsh, but I'd suggest you fix that stat. Or, you know, watch less Netflix and Discovery Channel."

"How did you . . . ?"

He cocked his head and studied her. "I see more than you think." Then he nodded toward the door and disappeared outside with his phone's flashlight on.

Now Sophie was the chicken, hiding inside while the guy she was fake dating, for-real crushing on, checked her house when she knew deep down it was all in her head.

Her therapist claimed that paranoia was a normal defense mechanism, to not feel bad about it. But every time Sophie peered over her shoulder only to find her own shadow chasing her, she felt less and less in control of her life.

It had taken all of her strength to leave him, to take the cash she'd hidden over the years in their basement—to start over. She had arrived on Nana's front porch in Crestler's Key with nothing but a tote bag full of cash and a new sense of pride.

Nana took her in with a warm hug, even though it had been three years since Sophie had seen her—which was so Sophie could protect the one person she loved. He didn't know Nana existed, didn't know to track Sophie to Crestler's Key. She would be safe here, get a new start.

And Sophie had done well here, despite everyone hating her. She'd counted that cash and discovered she'd saved three thousand dollars over the years, which wasn't massive wealth, but it had brought tears to Sophie's eyes all the same.

So when Nana mentioned that old Freddie Rochester was selling his farm for next to free, Sophie went to the bank, secured a loan, and scooped it up before the For Sale sign had been firmly stuck in the dirt.

She was living her life now, all on her own. Even though she still didn't have the right face shape. And it took smoothing three Aveda creams through her hair before it agreed to behave. And she had to choose A-line skirts instead of pencil ones to hide her baby-bearing hips. She was a stronger person now, flaws and all.

With a deep breath and a decision to forget the calls and the eerie feeling they conjured, Sophie went to the kitchen and grabbed a beer for Zac and another glass of wine for herself; if she planned to walk the buzz line, she might as well see it to the end.

Closing the refrigerator, Sophie turned back toward the family room to set out the drinks when she heard a loud *bang, bang, bang* on the back door. Startled, both the wine glass and beer bottle slipped from her grasp, and then a scream lodged in her throat as her mind jumped back to the day it all came to an end, the sounds of shattering glass as clear as day.

Her body shook violently, her eyes wide and her teeth clenched so tight that at first she didn't register that Zac was at the door, the laugh he'd released cut short by a look of concern.

"Hey . . . it's just me. Sophie, look at me."

Sophie, look at me.

She shook her head to clear the voice.

"It's me, Sophie. Look at me."

Look at me.

She closed her eyes to push back the fear building inside her. She was over this. Over it. Why couldn't her memories leave her alone?

"Sophie—"

"Stop!" And then, as though her own shout had yanked her back to the present, she started, her breathing heavy and her heart hammering. Sophie's hands shook as she covered her eyes, then ran them down her cheeks, and with all the control of a person seconds away from tears, dropped them back to her side. "I'm sorry."

But Zac was no longer by the back door. He must have freaked out and left.

Resigned, Sophie dropped to her knees to pick up the larger pieces of glass when strong hands eased around her arms and lifted her back up, fixing her to a chest that promised safety.

"It's okay." Zac's arms wrapped tighter around her, holding her to him. But it wasn't until he whispered in her ear that he wasn't going anywhere that the muscles in her body finally relaxed and she collapsed into him, her pride on the floor somewhere with the broken glass.

"I'm so sorry. I don't know what . . ."

"It's nothing. Just take a breath," he said, his arms still around her.

Sophie felt such intense contentment and comfort in his embrace that she didn't ever want to leave. Maybe she could ask him to hold her for a bit longer, just until the fear subsided, or maybe forever. But she knew she couldn't do that, not now and not ever.

So she lifted her head and prayed she hadn't started crying without realizing it.

"I'm sorry."

"It's okay. I shouldn't have scared you when you were already rattled. But then, something tells me it isn't me that's causing you to tremble right now." His gaze dropped to Sophie's hands, shaking so badly she looked like an addict who'd missed her last fix.

Quickly she tucked her hands into the back pockets of her jeans. "Cheap scare is all."

But Zac continued to watch her, not buying a lick of it. "All right. Well, why don't you go take a load off. I'll clean this up, get us some more drinks, and you can explain why you have crates in one corner of your family room and a wagon wheel in the other."

She grimaced. "Oh that."

"Yeah, see, I should have warned you that I have an epic problem. Serious personality flaw stuff here."

Sophie glanced purposefully from Zac's eyes to his toes and then back. "Yeah . . . not seeing it."

He laughed as he took a slow step toward her, biting his lip for effect and drawing Sophie's gaze there. Already she was relaxing, and the man had barely spoken to her. The way he made her feel safer without doing anything was unnerving.

"That's all superficial stuff. Real flaws live in here." He tapped his chest, dead center.

Sophie thought she had never met anyone who saw himself so clearly. If anything, Sophie suspected Zac was even better on the inside than on the outside. But she couldn't bring herself to say it, so instead she said, "Okay, I'm listening."

"See, that"—he pointed to the crates and then the wagon wheel—"is a problem for me. I'm a perpetual finisher. If I see an incomplete project, I have to finish it. It's like a complex puzzle dying to be solved, and I'm the crazy man who'll do the solving. So you go sit down, and I'll clean this up, and then you can explain to me how we can finish these projects tonight. Because I sure as hell can't leave here until they're done."

Sophie smiled at him, and he smiled back. For the first time, Sophie thought she might have gained a friend in Crestler's Key, other than Glenda.

Taking a seat in her family room, she watched as Zac grabbed the broom and dustpan and trash can from the pantry, all without asking where anything was stashed—as if he already understood her home and how he could fit in. And then he bent over to sweep it all up, and heaven help her. He turned around before Sophie could lift her gaze, and a wide smile broke across his face.

"Should I turn back around? Give you some additional viewing time?"

"What? I—no. I wasn't—no."

He winked. "Sure you weren't." Then he nodded toward the crates, saving her from more embarrassment. "Why don't you grab that stuff and bring it around to the couch? I'll be right there."

A strange feeling that she couldn't quite describe moved over Sophie, something that felt a lot like normalcy, but it had been far too long since she'd felt normal for her to be able to identify the feeling.

She pushed aside her current coffee table, which was one wrong move away from cracking a leg and falling apart, then brought around the four crates she'd brought home from the farm and a large sheet of plywood.

She set the crates on the floor, their light-colored wood bright against the dark wood floors. Then she laid out the sheet of plywood, the bolts, and the printouts of how to put the thing together.

After she had it all set out, she took a step back and stared at the apparent pile of junk just as Zac approached, his elbow brushing her arm, sending a flurry through her belly that made her far happier than it should have.

He scratched his head with his other arm. "So this is supposed to be . . . what exactly?"

"A coffee table."

His eyebrows shot up as he looked at her. "Seriously? Not like planters or something?"

"Nope, a coffee table. I thought you were Mr. Finisher."

"I finish. Every time." A glint of mischievousness flashed in his eyes, and then he laughed as her cheeks burned pink. "Sorry, I can't seem to help it around you. But I'll be good now."

"Seems to me you're always good." Their eyes met, and Sophie melted a little under his gaze. "You know, when you're not being an arrogant jerk."

He chuckled again. "Well, nobody's perfect, right?"

Right, only Sophie wasn't so sure that a certain farmer wasn't damn close.

"All right, so it's after eleven. You up for this?"

She nodded as she pointed at herself. "Night owl here. But what about you? Where's Carrie-Anne?"

"Tomorrow is a teacher workday, and she had a lesson at my sister's, so she's staying the night."

"What kind of lesson?"

"Riding."

"Hamilton Stables is into a little horse racing or something, right?"

Zac grinned. "I'm going to take you there so you can repeat that to them. Word for word, all right? I'd pay good money to see their reactions." He chuckled again. "But yeah, they do a little horse racing. Not sure if you follow the Triple Crown, but their horse won the Derby last year, won the Triple Crown a year or two ago as well. They're the best."

"Seems a little boring if you ask me. Who wants to be the best all the time?"

"Um . . . you?"

Sophie grimaced. "Point taken." And they laughed before sitting on the floor to go over the instructions.

"Do you have all the tools to do this?"

"Yeah, in the garage. I bought them when I decided I wanted to build this."

"You bought power tools so you could build a table? You know it would have been cheaper to buy a new coffee table, right?"

"Now what fun is that?" It was her turn to wink as she popped up and went to the garage, rummaged through the various tools she'd purchased over the last six months, and then returned with a power screwdriver. "Will this work?"

Zac looked impressed as he took the screwdriver from her. "Yeah, I'd say so."

For the next hour, they alternated between talking about nonsense and falling into a comfortable silence as they worked on the table, Zac occasionally directing Sophie to hold this or do that. More than once she found her eyes drifting his way, eager to watch the concentration on his face as he held a screw or bolt in his mouth while he fixed two pieces together, then screwed them together. She had suspected he would be handy, most farmers were, but watching it was something else entirely.

A few more minutes passed, and finally Sophie decided to ask the question she'd longed to ask since she first met Zac.

"So, I was wondering . . ."

He turned the table over and directed Sophie to hold one of the wheels in place so he could screw it to the base. "You were wondering what happened to Carrie's mom."

"I'm sorry. You probably get that all the time, don't you?"

"Yes," he said. Sophie feared she'd crossed the line, when he glanced over at her. "But I don't mind that you asked. She left."

Sophie's eyebrow knitted together in confusion. "What do you mean she left?"

"I mean just what I said. She left. Carrie-Anne was almost five years old, and Lora, her mom, woke me up, her bag all packed, and said she couldn't do it anymore—couldn't be a wife, a mom."

Pain crossed his face, and before Sophie thought better of it, she reached out and covered his hand with hers. His eyes dropped to the hand and then returned to Sophie. But she didn't say she was sorry or

ask him to go into more details. Sophie knew firsthand that sometimes the simple explanation was all a person could handle. And besides, did it really matter why his wife left? Or what happened that
led to her leaving? There was no world, no problem great enough for
Sophie to leave her daughter. Her heart broke for Carrie-Anne, a girl
so full of smiles you'd never know that she'd suffered such pain at
such a young age. Sophie wondered how much of it she remembered,
but knew she likely remembered it all.

Silence fell over them as they screwed another wheel into place,
and then Zac asked, "What about you? Ever married?"

Instantly, the image of herself at the courthouse flashed through
Sophie's mind, him beside her, an uneasiness to the moment that
shouldn't have been there. It should have been one of the happiest
days of her life.

She drew a breath and washed her face of any emotion, then told
the same lie she'd told every day since she left Merryville. "No.
Never married." She waited to see if he asked more, if he picked up
on the lie, but he simply nodded. They continued around the table,
fixing wheels into place until all four were secured to the base.

Zac picked up the table and set it down right side up. He spun it
around once to make sure the wheels worked and then grinned at Sophie. "One down."

Sophie squealed and clapped her hands. "It's perfect. Thank you
so much." She took a step and wrapped her arms around his neck,
hugging him close, the moment so full of happiness that she didn't
realize what she was doing until she pulled back, her eyes on his, a
new intensity in them.

"You're welcome." His head edged toward hers, his gaze flicking
to her mouth, then back to her eyes. An inch closer, and then his
warm breath hit her face. She swallowed, her nerves twisting, every
bone and muscle and fiber in her body screaming that she wanted
this, so desperately she wanted this.

But instead of Zac closing the distance, he squeezed her once
more, sending a zing of heat from his touch through her core, and
then took a step back, diverting his eyes.

He cleared his throat, ran a hand through his hair, before glancing
back at her. "It's late. I should probably . . ." He motioned to the
door, and she nodded, though inside she felt more than a little disappointment. What had just happened?

"Of course."

"Will you be all right?"

Sophie wasn't sure if he meant about the almost kiss or the phone calls earlier, but suddenly she could only think about one thing and it wasn't the random caller who refused to speak. "I'm fine."

"Okay then."

"Okay. Thank you again," she said. "It's perfect."

"Yeah, perfect," he said, his eyes on her. "See you Saturday."

"Saturday?"

Zac opened the door and smirked at her. "Our hot date, remember?"

A laugh broke free, but Sophie's mind had stopped working at "hot" and how perfectly it summed up how she felt inside and out. Hot. Like a fire had invaded her insides hot.

She swallowed hard. "Right. Hot date. See you tomorrow Zac."

Sophie closed the door behind him and then leaned against it, her thoughts racing to keep time with her heart. She wasn't sure what had happened between them tonight, but one thing was clear—there was nothing fake about her feelings for Zac Littleton. Nothing fake at all.

Chapter Eleven

Zac sat in his truck for nearly an hour, a part of him eager to cancel the date with Sophie, another part desperate to get to her, and the rest too confused to have an opinion. He'd never considered himself a fearful man; he was always willing to step up to the plate. To go the extra mile. To do whatever was needed of him. But something had happened last night when Sophie hugged him, and he couldn't right his reaction in his mind.

It was all so simple. They finished a project, she was thankful, and then she hugged him. And it should have ended there—a hug, a handshake, and a laugh, maybe another drink to celebrate. Whatever. But instead, her body pressed against his and his eyes closed for a moment and all he could think was *finally*.

In that moment, he would have given anything to pause time, to hold her there without the rest of the world ticking and moving around them. He could draw a long breath, take in her ocean scent, a scent that always brought him back to center. The likelihood of a woman possessing that specific scent as her natural smell seemed about as likely as winning the lottery. But there she was, in his arms, and then she pulled back and stared up at him, and every part of her—from the intensity in her eyes to the relaxed set of her mouth to the way her arms flexed around his neck—begged him to close the distance between them, to press his mouth to hers and find out what happened in the next chapter of their little story.

And he wanted to give in to her badly.

He let his guard down enough to ease into her and draw another breath, releasing it against her perfectly full lips, and then he remembered it all—Lora driving away, Carrie screaming after her—and he thought *no*. Whatever he was doing, he couldn't do that again.

Couldn't invite someone into their world, only to throw everything on its head again.

He could date casually, and he could flirt with Sophie. They could smile and laugh and do whatever the hell she needed to convince the town she wasn't the hateful person they'd conjured up in their heads. But he couldn't kiss her. That much he knew now. Because the moment he did, the moment he let himself taste her lips and feel her warmth, he knew with absolute certainty that he'd be all in. One hundred percent of his body and mind thrown at this person who had no idea what she'd opened up and very likely wouldn't be ready for it or want it. And then what?

Shit.

What the hell was he even doing here?

Zac started his truck for the second time, prepared to send a text and cancel the whole thing—give them both a little well-needed space to realign what they were doing—when he caught sight of her Mini Cooper coming down her dirt driveway.

Well, hell. No going back now.

Stepping out of his truck as she parked, Zac closed his door and pivoted slowly, a wall already forming around his heart. But then Sophie stepped out from her car with the most triumphant smile he'd ever seen on her face.

"Hey, you're early."

He shrugged. "Yet another one of those flaws I was telling you about."

Her smile spread, and he wondered if that excitement on her face was all for him. Surely not. "You seem happy."

She nodded slowly, like she was allowing the idea to settle over her. "Yeah . . . I guess I am. Seems to happen around you a lot lately." Her eyes met his, pure innocence within them, and just like that, his wall crumbled.

"I know the feeling."

They stared at one another, and Zac felt like a love-sick boy again, his heartbeat noticeable, his hands twitching slightly at his sides from the effort to keep from going to her, sweeping her into his arms, and claiming her mouth.

"You mind if I change real quick? I'm a mess," Sophie said, gesturing to her worn jeans and Fresh Foods tank top.

"I think you look great."

"You're just being nice."

"Unlikely."

She grinned in response.

The truth was he needed a minute to think so he could be around her without acting like an idiot. "But go change. I'll be out here."

"You can come in if you'd like."

"Nah, I'll just wait. But take your time."

She threw up an index finger and said, "I'll be one minute." Then she disappeared inside her house.

Zac released a long, long breath.

"She's just a girl," he said to himself. "No big deal." But as she returned wearing a simple pale yellow cotton dress and white sandals with her endless hair over her shoulders, he thought this woman wasn't just a big deal. She was a game changer.

"I like it," he said as he opened the passenger side door of his truck. "Though I'll warn you, I'm going to have a hard time concentrating now. I hope there's not a quiz after this date."

"No quiz, but you might be bored to death. We're going to Polly Farms outside of Gaffney."

"I've heard of it. What do you want to do there?"

"Research."

"On how to put them out of business? God, woman, are you trying to make enemies throughout all of America, or are you keeping it to the South?"

"I'm not trying to put them out of business. They're using some new technology that I'm considering for Fresh Foods. I just want to see it in action before I fork out the money."

Zac glanced over at her, impressed. "So legit research."

"That's what I said."

"So it is. And I'm your date for this because . . ."

"You look like you, and I hear Polly's weakness is younger men."

He choked on a laugh. "So you're whoring me out for profit. Gotcha. First lying, now this. You know Southern belles are supposed to be proper, right?"

Sophie winked at him. "Now, now, we both know true Southern women have no interest in being proper. They will flash you a smile while they plot your demise."

"So you *are* plotting to put them out of business."

"No! Aren't you listening? I'm researching how to better incorporate technology they are using."

"So you can outsell them."

"Well, yeah."

Zac chuckled. "How do I keep getting myself into these messes with you?"

"Because you can't resist my charm."

He pulled his eyes from the road to look at her. "Isn't that the damn truth."

Two hours later, Sophie had a complete understanding of rewilding, a new technique that was said to restore crops back to their wild, original forms prior to selective breeding.

"You realize it's unlikely you can call yourself organic if you have GMOs, natural or otherwise, right?" Zac asked.

"Well, I have to do something," Sophie said. "Organic farmers can't keep up with the productivity of farms like yours. This could change all that."

Zac wanted to argue against it, but it wasn't his business and he didn't want to sound like he knew more about farming than she did, especially about organic farming, which he'd never ventured into. So he continued to listen as they parked outside Polly's Farm for the U-Pick so they could see the fruit Polly had produced and compare it to what Fresh Foods had for the season.

"All right, so I have a very important question," Zac asked, stopping Sophie and turning her toward him.

"Which is?"

"Are we . . ." He leaned in closer, and Sophie tensed in anticipation, just as he'd hoped. Yeah, there was definitely chemistry between them. "Going to go on the hayride?"

She pushed him back. "Ugh. I thought you were going to . . ."

"Going to what?" His eyebrows went up in mock surprise, and she pushed him again, causing a laugh to break free.

"Nothing. Nothing at all. And yes. We're doing it all, so prepare to get your fun on. Because we're doing the petting zoo and the hayride, and if you aren't careful, I'll even make you go down that giant slide over there." She motioned to the kids play area to their right where, sure enough, a tall, inflatable slide led to a bouncy house.

"Yeah, not happening. But I'll go on the ride with you. Even hold your hand if you get scared in the woods."

"Funny."

"Which part?" He took a step toward her and closed his hand around hers, waiting for her reaction. But instead of pulling away, she threaded their fingers together and glanced up at him, curiosity on her face before that hint of fear he'd seen from time to time took shape.

"You know there's nothing to worry about here, right?"

"Here?"

"With me. I'm not as scary as I look." He squeezed her hand and held her gaze, asking her to trust him, though he hadn't figured out if he truly trusted her.

She swallowed hard but didn't look away. He thought she might laugh it off, but then she said, "To me, you . . . this . . . isn't scary. It's terrifying."

A soft breeze blew past them, ruffling Sophie's hair and locking Zac to her and this moment. "I know, but it doesn't have to be."

"No?"

"No."

"But, see, I don't know how . . ."

He lifted a finger to her lips, silencing her. "Me either, but maybe we can figure it out together. Maybe we don't need to know the how right now, just the why. And for me, I . . ." He shook his head and ran a hand through her hair, tucking the loose strands behind her ear. "I can't stay away."

"So the fake stuff?"

"Isn't so fake for me."

For a second, Zac thought he'd revealed too much too soon, his mouth speaking faster than his brain could keep up. But just as he opened his mouth to backpedal, she said, "Well, then, let's get this date started before all the best strawberries are picked."

"Yeah?"

"Yeah."

"Lead the way then, madam."

She tugged his hand, and he went where she led, that inkling of doubt speaking up that he should hold back, keep all his cards a little closer. But he'd been doing that for years now, and what did he have to show for it? Nothing and no one. So it was time to try something else, and if he landed on his face, then so be it.

It wouldn't be the first time he'd crawled out of a grave and found a way to live again.

"Can we pick strawberries first? I've never picked them like this."

"You've never been to a U-Pick?"

She shook her head.

"But what about at Fresh Foods?"

"Sure, I've checked them and helped the staff before, but a real U-Pick feels like a competition, you know? Who can fill her basket first? Who finds the biggest berry? It's just fun."

"I had no idea you were so competitive."

Sophie beamed. "You're looking at the national high school chess champion. Three years in a row."

"Chess, really?"

"Hey, I won the spelling bee, too."

He broke into laughter, and she play punched him. "What? Is Mr. Athlete making fun of the nerd? Well, I got into every college I applied to. What about you? How far did those muscles take you?"

Zac almost answered with the truth—that he had received four full rides from major colleges, two in football, two in baseball. But as he took in that sassy look on her face, her hands on her hips, he couldn't bring himself to say it. So instead he said, "Gotta admit, I'm pretty impressed. You still play?"

"Occasionally."

"Maybe you could teach me sometime. See if I could go up against the champion. But for now, you've got your hands full because, see, I run my very own U-Pick. I know how these berries grow and where the best berries are hidden. So I'll go ahead and apologize now because you're about to get waxed."

She took a step closer, her game face firmly in place. "Is that right? Because if farming has taught me anything, it's that no two seasons are the same and no two farms produce in the same way. So I'm thinking we should put a little money on it. You know, unless you're afraid to lose."

"That didn't exactly go so well for you last time."

Her eyes narrowed, and Zac tossed up his hands with a laugh. "Sorry, couldn't help it."

"Yeah, you'll be sorry when I destroy your ass."

"We'll see." He paid for their two baskets, handed one to her, and then eyed the strawberry patch before glancing her way. "You ready?"

"Born ready."

He smiled again. "Fair enough. Winner gets to pick the next date."

"A little overconfident, don't you think? Who says you're getting another date?"

His gaze switched to her and stayed there, fixing her to the spot. "Aren't I?"

The corners of Sophie's mouth curved up the tiniest bit, and he found himself wishing he could press a soft kiss to that very spot. "Yes, I guess you are."

"All right. On your mark." He eyed her again. "Get set." Sophie took the runner's pose. "Go!"

They both dashed into the strawberry patch, nearly knocking over innocent children, which sent them both into fits.

"I'm taking this one, Littleton."

"We'll see."

And then it was on. For the next half-hour, Zac alternated between picking berries and watching Sophie, a thousand details popping out now, when just days before they'd been unimportant. The way she giggled when she found her first berry. The way she talked animatedly to herself the entire time. The way her face lit up when she passed an especially large berry to a little boy who looked as though she'd just given him a prize egg on Easter Sunday.

If not for the fact that he knew it would upset her if he let her win, he'd have sat on the grassy bank, ditched the strawberry picking, and watched her work, that glow of hers touching every person she passed, until half the people in the patch were in on her hunt, helping her, finding more and more berries. In minutes she'd created a team of people willing to sacrifice their berries for her, asking for nothing in return but her charm. And, hell, he couldn't blame them. Her charm had hypnotized him long ago.

Finally, she rushed up to him, her basket overflowing. "I'm full, and I demand a count."

"You had help."

"No one said that was against the rules. You could have asked for help."

"Like any of them were going to help me when a pretty blonde is the opponent."

She grinned and bounced on the balls of her feet, too excited to contain it. "Let's count. Hurry."

Zac glanced over to spy several people watching them, waiting to see if she'd won, they as invested as she was. And dear God, he was hooked. Absolutely hooked. How a person could affect strangers so easily was beyond him, but she had—she did, on a constant basis. And he realized then it really was he who was standing in her way in Crestler's Key. They wouldn't support her out of loyalty to him. Well, enough of that. It was time the town appreciated the wonder that was Sophie Marsh.

The older man running the entrance booth walked over. "I've got a scale here if y'all want to do a weight."

"Perfect," Sophie said, unable to remain still.

The man took her basket and then Zac's, weighed each, and turned to the crowd who'd formed around them. "And the winner is . . ." He leaned closer to Sophie, and she whispered her name. "Sophie!"

The crowd exploded in applause and cheers, and Zac pretended to be disappointed. But actually, he was buzzing inside, happy in a way he hadn't been in a long, long time.

"Hayride now?" he asked, eager to surprise her with a little detour.

"Definitely."

The crowd from the strawberry patch had lined up beside a tractor with a trailer attached to it, bales of hay arranged along the railing for people to sit on during the ride.

"Up you go," Zac said, lifting Sophie easily onto the trailer and then stepping up himself to sit down beside her, his legs hanging off the edge.

"You're pretty strong, you know that?"

He peered over his shoulder. "Something tells me you are, too."

She held his stare, and Zac thought he could get used to this. Someone beside him, a feminine touch to his hard shell. Someone to remind him that life didn't have to be lonely.

"Wow, it's peaceful," Sophie said as they set out through the rows of trees in the orchard. Zac took her hand, rubbing his thumb slowly back and forth, enjoying the feel of her small hand in his.

"I like this," he said, and she smiled.

"The hayride."

"You."

Her smile softened as she peered up at him. "Yeah . . . me, too."

Zac wrapped an arm around her, holding her close, as they continued through the orchard, past the cow pastures, to the barn in the far back where they stopped for some lemonade and cookies.

"And this is us." Zac hopped off the edge and held out his hand for Sophie to join him.

She glanced at the trailer, still packed with people enjoying their plastic cups of lemonade and small cellophane bags of cookies. "But no one else is getting off."

"Special detour."

"Um . . . what kind of detour?"

"The surprise kind. Now hurry up before Tim starts the tractor again."

She placed her hands on her hips in that cute Sophie way. "And how exactly do you know his name?"

Zac winked at her. "Not my first time here."

"Are you for real? Why didn't you say something?"

He shrugged. "You were excited. And besides, I've never been to their U-Pick. Just the main farm."

"Because you're friends with the owner or something?"

Zac took her hand and directed her to the left. "Not me. My dad fought in Vietnam with Charlie Smith, Polly's husband."

"Charlie . . ."

"Yeah, my brother was named after him."

"So they don't just know each other, random barely-know-each-other kind of Southern friends, but are real friends."

"I'd say they're like brothers. They fought together. That kind of thing stays with a man."

Sophie tossed up her hands. "Brothers! God, you must have thought I was such an idiot to bring you here."

"Not at all. Like I said, I've never been to their U-Pick."

"Well, I'm voiding this date in the books. I get to pick the next date, too."

He smirked. "You won the picking contest, remember?"

"The next two dates then."

"Two dates? Now look who's so sure of herself."

"Oh, you're going on two more dates with me whether you like it or not. You can ditch me after that if you'd like, but I get to plan two distinct dates, and they are going to be doozies, and you're going to—Oh my God."

She covered her mouth with her hands, her eyes wide as they stepped out from the protection of the forest to the small lake before them, nature cradling it in pink and yellow and lavender flowers, like something out of a dream. In the middle of the lake, a family of ducks paddled along, oblivious to their presence, and Zac wished he'd thought to bring bread.

"The Smiths added the dock since I was here last," Zac said, pointing to the dock and the small johnboat tied to it. "But otherwise, it looks just as I remember it."

"It's beautiful. Unbelievably beautiful. Did they plant the flowers?"

"No, they're wild. The Smiths try to maintain them, but this is all natural, nothing about it manufactured. Just nature."

"You did it without even trying."

"Did what?"

"Trumped my date."

"To me, you already won. You should have seen the look on your face when you were picking berries and gave the biggest one to that little boy. He lit up, and you were so excited for him. That was the best part of the date for me."

"But that was nothing. Just common kindness."

"You don't realize how rare it is. There's nothing common about it. It comes so naturally to you that it's second nature. But to most people? To me? It's harder. We have to work on it, constantly think about the right thing to do. But not you. It's a part of your very being." Then Zac nodded toward the dock. "Walk out here with me." He took her hand again, sure he would never grow bored of holding her hand, of the way she tightened her grasp as they walked. Like she was afraid he might pull away.

They walked out to the edge of the dock and stared out over the lake, the sun beginning its decline behind the trees, everything calming down as another day inched closer to its end.

"Why did you buy the farm? Of all the things you could do, why that?"

"Do you want the truth?"

"Always."

"I'd been into organic foods for a long time and the whole 'taking things back to their basics' and getting rid of fillers that were causing cancer and God could only guess what else. It was interesting to me. Still is. But I never had an opportunity to produce my own, to put all of those years of research to good use, until one day my life changed. I moved to Crestler's Key and saw that Freddie was selling his farm for a bargain price. It felt fated."

"So you bought the farm because you're passionate about organic food?"

She stood taller and kept her gaze fixed on something across the lake, her demeanor changing before his eyes. Like some thought or memory had invaded the moment.

"You don't have to talk about—"

"I bought it because I needed to find myself. I needed to remember that I was a real, living breathing person. That I mattered. That my wants for my life mattered. I needed something that was all me, my two hands, and if it failed, it failed, but at least I tried to do it all on my own." She sucked in a breath and glanced down.

Zac couldn't wait another second.

He took her hand, causing her to look up, those startling blue eyes searching him—Zac, someone she barely knew—for comfort and support. Like she was a little girl so desperately in need of approval that she'd accept it from anyone. It broke him, broke through all the doubts and chaos in his mind, all the reasons he'd given himself to stay away. Because although he might not be inherently kind, he was a good person, and he could sense when someone needed something to keep them from falling over the edge. And Sophie Marsh didn't need just anything.

She needed him.

With one final exhale to release the last of his uncertainty, Zac edged closer to her, pulling her to him at the same time, two magnets finding their attraction. He glided his hands over her cheeks, shaking his head slowly as he took in her beautiful face. Then, with the ducks as their only witnesses, he pressed his lips to hers, his hands gently cradling her face as she rose up to him, embracing the kiss. Embracing him and his silent promise to be what she needed. Even if eventually what she needed was for him to say good-bye.

And with that realization, the kiss intensified, him securing her to his chest, her hands in his hair, their mouths and tongues saying all the things they hadn't been brave enough to say before. That they wanted each other, deeply, in ways neither was prepared to explore. Emotionally and physically, Zac could no longer deny that they were meant to be more than enemies. More than friends. More than fake dating. They were meant to be together.

With a sigh, Sophie pulled away, her eyes still closed. Zac kissed her cheek, then her forehead, then her lips once more because he couldn't resist even if he'd tried.

"Let me help you."

Her eyes opened. "Help me what?"

"I'm not the one who can answer that. You are. But I'm here. Whatever you need. If it's this . . ." He kissed her again, this time tasting her lips, feeling his own tingle after he pulled away. "Then I'm here. If it's friendship, then I can do that, too."

She glanced up slowly at him. "I don't want to be your friend."

"No?"

"No. I want . . ." Her hands glided over his arms, around his neck, into his hair. She smiled a little. "I've been wanting to do that since the first time I met you."

"Touch my hair?"

"Kiss you."

His heart stilled, and he thought that this was what life was about— these quiet moments that were so often rushed.

He leaned in and kissed her again, then held her to him, her heart beating against his chest as they watched the sun slip behind the trees, the day ending, but the start of something else blooming on the horizon.

Chapter Twelve

Sophie rolled the wagon wheel away from the wall where it had rested for the last month and a half to the middle of her family room, then placed her hands on her hips and stared at it. A Miranda Lambert song played in the background, intensifying Sophie's get-it-done mood.

"You and me, wheel. I hope you're ready for this because you're getting owned tonight. See, I have a finisher in my life now, and I can't just go around leaving stuff started when he's around, now can I? Nope. So, you? You're going on my wall when I get back . . . even if I have no idea how I'll lift you up there. But it's happening. Tonight."

Tonight.

The thought made Sophie giddy. There would be a tonight, a plan that involved more than just her and a glass of wine and an episode of *Fixer Upper*. And although she'd been just fine in that world, she was ready to see what life felt like when there was more to it than a singular wake up and an empty good night.

So she was going to finish this wheel, and not because Zac would judge her if she didn't, but because it was time. In fact, it was time for a lot of things.

Heading into her bedroom, she studied the bare space over her headboard and decided she needed to get a stud finder just to be safe. Maybe Zac would have one, and then he could show her how to use it so she wouldn't have to search on YouTube or google instructions.

The thought made her smile anew. She had someone in her life now to help with these things, to teach her how to do this or that. Someone to lean on and someone who could lean on her. It was a strange thing, and a part of her wanted to take a step back, to realize that this, whatever it was between them, was new and could end any moment. But if Nana's illness had taught Sophie anything, it was that time was precious. For now, this tiny moment, she intended to enjoy the *whatever* happening between her and Zac Littleton.

And because she would see Zac at the market very soon, she could ask him about the stud finder. You know, while she sat across from him, trying to sell things instead of staring at him. Just like the last time they were at the market together, because he'd been right all those weeks ago—she had intentionally positioned herself across from him. And now a month later, the spot was still reserved, thanks to her agreement to give the mayor a fresh apple pie and a half dozen lemon tarts.

She bit her lip as she thought of seeing Zac there, her mind going back to their kiss and how perfectly she fit against him, cradled there, nothing to worry about.

Surely happiness couldn't be this simple, but Sophie couldn't bring herself to think about all the ways this could blow up in her face. Not yet. That would come, but for now, she intended to be happy.

Besides, it was high time she worry less over all the things that'd once plagued her and embrace the person she was today, mind and . . . body.

So instead of pulling out a long skirt or dress, something to cover the long scar on her left knee that had been there since she was a little girl but had been a problem for someone else, so she wasn't permitted to show it, she slid on a pair of white shorts and a royal blue sleeveless top. Then she slipped on wedge sandals to bring her up a few inches because her legs were too short to balance out her pear shape, so she needed to—

No.

Slowly, Sophie stepped out of the wedges and replaced them in her closet, then pulled out the pretty flat sandals she'd found on sale but hadn't worn because at five-two she was too short to pull them off. But why? Why couldn't she wear flat shoes and shorts? Why couldn't she embrace her shortness and scars?

She could—would. Starting today.

With her new outfit set, she drew a long breath and turned to look at herself in her floor-length mirror. A smile stretched across her face, and she closed her closet door before her brain could pick apart her outfit and all of her imperfections. For once she didn't care if her hair was just right, her makeup highlighting her attributes and hiding her mole. No, for once she was just herself, and that had to be enough.

A surge of pride worked through her core, followed immediately by nervousness because she'd never stepped out of her house without checking her teeth to make sure they weren't smudged with lipstick or that her concealer hadn't creased below her eyes. What if . . .

You're fine.

Before she could talk herself out of it, she grabbed her bag and closed her front door. Glenda and the two boys from Fresh Foods she'd hired for the summer would be there by now, and she didn't want them to do everything. The market would be crowded, perhaps even more crowded than it had been two weeks ago, and they would need to be fully stocked to keep up.

Sophie parked in a vendor spot and took the cobblestone walkway that led to the circular center of the market, then she dashed toward her booth. As she feared, most of the booths were already set up.

"There you are," Glenda called as she approached.

Although everything in her ached to glance over to see if Zac was there yet, Sophie forced herself to focus on her staff first. They were there to help her on a Saturday, and that kind of dedication deserved her full attention.

She edged behind the Fresh Foods booth, careful not to bump the displays. "Sorry, running late this morning. But it looks like everything's set up already."

Glenda smiled. "It is. We had some help."

"Good. I asked Kirk and Sam to stop by, and they said they would. Glad they made it here before me."

"No, not them. Him."

Sophie followed Glenda's outstretched finger to the booth across from theirs where a certain farmer was loading baskets on his table. His hair gleamed in the morning sunlight, showing flecks of blond in the brown, and his tanned arms flexed as he lifted a crate of apples. As usual, he was wearing a Littleton Farms T-shirt and jeans, and Sophie found herself staring far longer than appropriate.

"Zac helped you?"

"Yep. He parked beside me and offered to help carry things in, then ended up carrying it all in himself while I set up."

"That's . . ." Sophie couldn't pull her eyes away from him. Then, as though he felt her stare, he stilled mid-motion while placing a basket on his table and turned his head, his gaze hitting hers dead on.

She lifted her hand in a small hello, and he grinned a hello back.

"Thank you," she called out.

"Any time," he said, his voice low, both staring at each other like fools. Sophie wished she could go over to him, see if he would pull her forward and kiss her as he had the day before. But maybe that was all normal-ish stuff for him, and they were back to being enemies. This was uncharted territory for her, and she feared that doing anything might mess it all up. So she continued to stare, until she realized that someone was calling her name. Loudly.

"Sophie!"

Her trance broke, and Sophie glanced around. "What? What happened?"

"You tell me. Kirk and Sam are here now, and I didn't know if you needed them to do anything, so I was asking you, but you were in a Zac daze. Wow, when did this happen?"

Sophie said hello to the two boys who worked at the farm part time, then asked them to grab the extra Fresh Foods baskets and bags from the van. After they were out of sight, she focused on her friend, her mind mud, her legs Jell-O after the stare fest with Zac.

"When did what happen?"

"You and Zac. First he all but ditches his own staff to help me, and then you're staring at each other like you're ready to rip the other one's clothes off."

"We were not."

"You were. And he's still staring."

Sophie glanced over to find Zac smiling at her before going back to work, and then she was smiling again, too.

"Okay, that smile is not nothing. Spill it before I die here. What are you doing with Zac Littleton? And furthermore, and maybe more important, how many tattoos are we talking about here? On his chest? His back? I need details please."

"What? I don't know."

"So you're not that far into it? Fair enough. But you've kissed?"

"I . . . we . . ." Sophie bit her lip, and Glenda jumped up and down.

"I knew it! You kissed Zac Littleton!"

"Dude, you didn't tell us you kissed her."

Sophie spun around to find Charlie and Brady standing between their booth and Fresh Foods's, Zac's head dropped in aggravation as the brothers asked a thousand questions as though she weren't standing right behind them.

And then she realized it wasn't merely the Littleton brothers who'd picked up on the conversation. Annie-Jean and Patty were both staring her way. The mayor was outside Zac's booth, questioning him on what this meant for the town, while Rick went on about who he should stock at the grocery store if she and Zac were to get married.

Finally Zac shook his head, and she thought for sure he was regretting the whole thing when he said, "Screw it. You want answers? Here're your answers."

He hopped over his booth and started for hers with purpose, his face so tense she considered backing up. He leaned over her table and took her face in his hands, his mouth covering hers before she could ask what he was doing. For a moment she tensed, but there was no denying her body's response to him. She gripped his shoulders and pulled him toward her, but in her damn flats, she couldn't reach him properly. So she did the only thing she could—she climbed onto the table, every part of her desperate to be closer to this man.

Not a thought went through her mind of where they were or who might be watching until she finally pulled away and her gaze dropped to the table, her on her knees, her chest pressed firmly to Zac's, and he released a deep laugh that rumbled through both of them.

"I'd say that about settles it. This"—Zac pointed between himself and Sophie—"is a thing now. Just thought y'all should know."

"So this a thing now, huh?" Sophie asked playfully as she turned down her street, her phone pressed to her ear, a smile fixed in place since their kiss at the market.

Instantly, Glenda had demanded to know everything, and Sophie assured her she would divulge . . . as soon as she figured it all out herself.

Something demanding Zac's attention had happened at Littleton Farms, so he had to leave the market before they could have a real conversation, but he promised that they would talk tonight. Except Sophie had never been the patient sort, which was why it took less than ten minutes after leaving the market for her to crack and call Zac, eager to hear his voice.

"Didn't you hear? It's big news. All over town, in fact."

"Is that right?"

"I'm afraid so."

"And what does this being a thing stuff involve exactly?"

"A little of this, a little of that. Kissing required, clothes optional."

She laughed. "Forever the flirt."

"Only with you."

Her heart warmed as she parked outside her house and tapped her keys against her steering wheel, wishing their date was right now instead of hours from now. "So your place."

"My place. I'm doing the cooking thing. Prepare to be wowed."

"Really? I didn't realize you cooked."

"I'm a farmer."

"So am I, and there's no fancy cooking to be had here."

"You cook."

"Oh no, I bake. Big difference."

"Ah, I see." Then Sophie heard someone calling for Zac, and he said he had to run before reluctantly hanging up.

Now she had two hours to kill and no idea what to do to fill the time.

Then she thought of the wheel that still needed to be chalk painted and distressed and then waxed, so maybe she could do that to fill the time and prove she was indeed changing.

With resolve, she started for her front door, just as a text from Zac came through.

So, I'm thinking a slasher movie tonight. Research how many times they call and hang up before attacking. Thoughts?

She laughed and started to text back when her gaze caught on the bright green vase of overflowing wildflowers sitting on her front porch.

Wildflowers.

I hate wildflowers. Real flowers are more delicate. Like a rose. You might be a wildflower now, but trust me, soon we'll turn you into a rose.

A tremor moved down her back as goose bumps popped across her skin. It couldn't be. He didn't know she was here, didn't know how to find her. She was safe.

But she couldn't shake the feeling that she'd been a fool.

Picking up the flowers, she read the card: *For being a nice girl.*
Nice girl?

Then it clicked—Zac. He'd commented yesterday on her being nice, so he must have sent these and the note as a joke. That had to be it.

She quickly pulled Zac's text back up and sent her own.

Nice girl, huh? We'll see about that. P.S. Thanks for the flowers.

She clicked Send, then unlocked her door and went inside, her heart growing lighter with each step. Zac had sent her flowers, something she hadn't received in a long, long time. More and more, she thought maybe this would be different. Maybe—

Her phone pinged with a new text, and she set the vase on her kitchen counter. She picked up the phone and read the text, only to have the phone slip from her grasp, clinking against the granite countertop.

Flowers? Not me, though I'm a little disappointed that I didn't think of it first. Guess I'm not your only admirer.

Sophie peered at the flowers, so innocent in their vase, and immediately rushed over, grabbed the card, then turned it over to find the name of the florist who'd delivered them. With trembling hands, she dialed the number and waited, her heart picking up speed, a thousand thoughts running away in her mind.

"Truth's Gold Florist."

"Hi there, I was hoping you could help me. I just received flowers, but there's no name listed on the card for me to offer my thanks. Can you tell me who sent them?" Sophie's voice was rattling, but she couldn't force it to even out. Not until she knew.

The florist was from a neighboring town, so not directly local, which meant this could be from a customer who'd been by the farm. Sophie often tossed in extras with each of her orders, and she liked to randomly send baskets to the hospital for the nurses who worked such long hours and rarely received the thanks they deserved. There could be a logical explanation.

"Sure, let me see what I can find for you. What's your name?"

Sophie rattled off her name and address, while praying that it was just a customer. Just a thankful nurse from the hospital. Anything or anyone other than him.

"I'm sorry. There's no name listed, and the person paid with cash."

Cash. So he couldn't be tracked.

No. Stop freaking yourself out, Sophie.

"Okay, thank you."

"Of course."

She hung up and paced her small kitchen in search of answers. Again, maybe it was someone offering the same anonymous gift to her that she did to others. But why couldn't she stop shaking?

Her phone rang in her hand, and she dropped it again, this time onto the hardwood. "Ugh." Her new iPhone now had an impressive crack in the display. She reached to pick it up just as her home phone rang, and her eyes drifted up slowly. The phone continued to ring—long, painful cries—but Sophie couldn't bring herself to answer the call. Because if no one answered, if she heard nothing but that blood-curling scraping sound, she might fall apart right this second. And she was stronger than the Sophie who fell apart . . . she had to be.

She waited until the phone stopped ringing, then unplugged it from the wall, taking away her temptation to answer it and confirm her fears.

The wheel, focus on the wheel. But she couldn't shake the feeling that she was being watched—someone inside her house or out, eyes on her, was watching her every move.

Her cell pinged again with a text, and she reluctantly picked it up, only to release a breath of relief.

Can you come over a little early? Carrie wants you to do her nails.

She grabbed her bag from the kitchen barstool, her keys from the counter, and quickly typed back:

On my way.

Chapter Thirteen

"Dad, I need the nail polish remover."

"In your bathroom, right side of the vanity."

"How about cotton balls?"

"Right beside it."

Zac shook his head as he realized how much he knew about nail polish and the things needed to remove it. There was a time when he'd have looked dumbfounded if someone had asked him how to remove the stuff, but he'd done it himself too many times to count now, always eager to fill the mother gap for Carrie.

But today, she hadn't asked for his help. She'd glanced at her sandaled feet, her hair in a ponytail she'd fixed in place herself, because he'd never been good at that kind of thing, and asked if he thought Sophie might be willing to help her. He said of course, even before he'd texted Sophie, knowing she would be happy to help, and now she was headed over, invading their world.

So far the only real interaction they'd all had together was those few minutes before his and Sophie's first date. But this would be different, and he wondered how Carrie would take it—if she'd wonder what would come of this and what that would mean for her.

"Hey, got a second?" he asked just before she disappeared down the hallway.

"Yeah. Need help boiling water?"

He grinned. "Very funny."

"I thought so," she said, so much his kid it hurt.

"Well, I wanted to ask, you know, what you think of this?"

She studied him. "You mean your outfit? I don't know . . . seems a little casual, but I don't know what women like Sophie like. Does she like casual?"

"Not the outfit. The date itself."

"What do you mean?"

With a long sigh, Zac turned down the stove eye and walked around the kitchen island to stand before his daughter. "I mean, do you have questions? Are you worried? You know you are my top priority, no matter what, right? That no one will ever come between you and me."

"I know. But I like Sophie. I like that she's going to be around. She's nice, and she's very pretty. I'm thinking she could teach me how to do makeup."

Zac choked on his next words and began coughing. "Makeup?"

"I'm getting older, Dad, and most of the girls wear a little."

Twelve-year-olds wear makeup now? Before he knew it, they'd be having conversations about bras, then dating. He needed a drink. And a class or six on how to handle a preteen girl.

"Well, Aunt Kate could help with that."

"I know. But she's busy a lot, and I'd like to . . ."

"To what?"

Carrie-Anne shrugged her small shoulders and peered up at her dad. "Have my own person to ask, you know?"

"Oh." A pang of hurt surged through him, but before he could dwell on it, the doorbell rang, and Carrie took off running to get it. "She's here!"

So much for Carrie not becoming invested. She already had hope that this would become something more, and he'd just started seeing Sophie. But then again, the truth of it was . . . so did he.

The door opened, and Sophie stood there still in the same shorts and blouse she had on at the market, her face pale, nothing about her resembling the happy person he'd seen earlier.

"Sophie!" Carrie said, wrapping her arms around her, only for Sophie to flinch and then realize who was in her arms.

"Hey, sweetie. How are you?" She threw on a smile that Zac knew wasn't anywhere near her real smile and ran a hand over Carrie's hair, then hugged her again. "It's good to see you again."

Carrie took Sophie's hand and dragged her in, closing the door behind her, but Sophie still hadn't looked at Zac.

"Hey, Carrie, why don't you run and grab the nail stuff."

"Good idea. Be right back," she said, beaming at Sophie.

As soon as his daughter was out of sight, Zac walked over to Sophie. "What's wrong?"

She drew a rattled breath, then another that didn't seem to help. "Nothing. I just . . . nothing."

He took her hands and threaded his fingers through hers, then glanced down at them. "You're shaking."

Sophie swallowed and lowered her head. "I'm sorry. I just got a little freaked out earlier. Shook me to the bones and I can't seem to clear it from my head."

"Freaked out how? The slasher call again?" he joked, but he immediately realized that there was nothing funny about it. She wasn't just scared—she was petrified.

"You're okay, you know that, right? You're here. Nothing's going to hurt you here."

She nodded, and he pulled her to him, hugging her close in hopes of calming her down, his mind racing to figure out what had happened in her past to create this level of fear. Had someone broken into her house when she was a child? Had she been held at gunpoint at a gas station? What happened to make her this afraid of her own shadow?

"I'm sorry. Really, I'm fine."

"Sophie . . ."

She glanced up, and he leaned away from her so he could try to decipher what was going on in her head, but she wasn't giving anything away. "You know you can talk to me about it if you need to."

"I know."

Yet he could tell she had no intention of talking about it. At least not today.

"Here it is," Carrie said, busting back into the room with all the excitement of a typical twelve-year-old. "I can do yours, too, if you'd like."

Sophie separated from Zac and went to his daughter, then she put on a smile and relaxed her body so as not to worry Carrie. Once again, he was impressed with how often she put others before herself.

"Let's do yours first, and then if there's time, you can do mine. Sound good?"

"Sounds great. I'm going to Margaret-May's house in an hour, and we're supposed to have matching nails. Orange." Carrie held up the orange polish Zac had picked up for her on his way home from the farm.

"Oooh. Pretty. Do you have any glitter?"

"Glitter?"

Sophie flashed a mischievous smile. "I'm going to tell you a secret, but you have to promise not to tell anyone."

"I promise. What is it, what is it?"

She leaned in closer and whispered, "If you sprinkle glitter onto your polish before it dries, you can turn any polish into glitter polish. Want to try it?"

"Yes! Be right back." Carrie dashed back down the hall to grab glitter, and Zac thought it wasn't possible to adore the woman any more than he did already, but somehow she'd surpassed his expectations again.

"Thank you."

She grinned over at him, the gesture not quite reaching her eyes, and he wished she would tell him what was going on so he could help her. So he could fix it. "For what?"

"For being you."

She smiled again, and then Carrie was back and they dove into the nail thing while he continued with dinner.

Thirty minutes later, Carrie had sparkly orange nails, and they were all seated at the table for grilled chicken Alfredo and Italian salad, the dressing made from scratch, thanks to his mom's recipe that never failed to impress.

They ate while Carrie talked away about horseback riding lessons and gymnastics and whether she should try out for cheerleading. Although Sophie asked questions and generally acted as though it were the most interesting conversation she'd ever had, Zac could tell she was still shaken by whatever had happened before she arrived.

He tried to think if she'd said something, anything, that might be a clue, and then he remembered the text about the flowers.

"Hey, did you figure out who your secret admirer is?" Zac asked with a smile that quickly dropped away when he caught the look on her face.

"Someone sent you flowers?" Carrie asked. "How nice. Dad, you should send Sophie flowers."

"Yeah, I should. Hey kiddo, why don't you grab your bag. The Pattersons will be here any second to pick you up."

Zac waited for Carrie-Anne to clean off her plate in the trash, slip it into the dishwasher, and disappear down the hall to grab her overnight bag before he returned his focused to Sophie, unable to hold back any longer. Sophie was a confident woman who liked her independence, so he didn't want to come across as overbearing, but she was obviously frightened. What kind of man would he be if he didn't at least try to help?

"Okay, spill it," he said, likely too forceful, but he couldn't help it. Worry had taken over. "What happened before you came here? Why do you look like you saw a ghost?"

She offered a weak smile. "Sort of feels like I did."

Just then the doorbell rang and Carrie shouted that she was coming. She gave Zac a hug, and he kissed her cheek before they opened the door and she refused to let him baby her, then they said hello to Margaret-May, who'd run up to their door to get Sophie.

"Love you, kiddo. Call if you need anything," Zac called as the girls ran off to the Pattersons' SUV.

He waited until the taillights were long disappeared down the road before closing the door and turning back to Sophie.

"Here's the thing. I'm standing right here, and I want to help you, but I can't do a thing if you don't trust me enough to tell me what's going on."

"It's not about trust." She sat down on the sofa and clasped her hands in her lap. "Don't you have things in your life that you'd rather forget than talk about? Where talking about them brings up all those old memories, and they last long after the conversation's over? Well, I don't want to remember. Isn't there anything you don't want to remember?"

He thought of when he came home to find another man in his bed with Lora and knew just what she meant.

"I do. Lots of things in fact. But if it's impacting your present self, then you might need to deal with it if you really want to move on."

"See that's the thing. I thought I had. But then . . ." She trailed off as she tucked her legs up under her and stared into his family room, her gaze locking on a photo of Carrie and Zac at Disney World three years ago. "She's wonderful, you know? You've done an amazing job with her."

"Thank you."

"Really, her enthusiasm is infectious."

"So is yours . . . usually." Her eyes lifted to his, and he walked over, sat beside her, and pulled her legs into his lap. "I don't want you to be afraid here."

"I'm not afraid here."

"Good because—"

"I'm afraid everywhere."

Zac's words caught in his throat. "Everywhere? But why?"

Sophie sat back against the couch, her thoughts inward. "I used to be a different person than I am now. In a bad place. And I met someone who made it worse. We ended things." Her eyebrows went up. "Or I ended things. He didn't take it very well."

"And you think he's the one who's been calling you? The one who sent the flowers?"

"I don't know."

"Are you afraid of him—afraid he'll hurt you?"

Her gaze drifted away again, and Zac felt every overprotective bone in his body tensing, ready for a fight. Yet he had no idea who he was up against.

"You don't have to talk about it, but I'm not comfortable with you going home alone tonight."

"I'll be fine."

"Either you stay here and I'll sleep on the couch, or I'll be forced to sleep in my truck outside your house. Doesn't matter to me— okay, that's a lie. I'd rather you just stay here, but if you won't listen to reason, then I'll just have to stalk your door."

She smiled for the first time. "You'd do that?"

"Absolutely."

"Or I could stay here?"

"Or you could stay here."

"I don't have a toothbrush."

"I have a spare."

"And what I would sleep in?"

Zac stood and went into his room, returning with a light blue Littleton Farms T-shirt, the logo in white—it was his favorite.

"You can sleep in this."

"And I'd sleep . . . here?" She pointed at the couch, and suddenly it occurred to Zac that she was here, alone with him in his house.

"In my bed."

Her eyes locked on his, and she swallowed hard. "I'll sleep out here. I can't take your bed." And Zac couldn't be sure, but he thought he saw disappointment cross her face. "But . . . if it's okay with you . . . I think I'd like to stay here."

"Then it's settled." He went over to the end table, grabbed the remote, and passed it to her. "You choose the movie, I'll pop the popcorn."

He started away when she called out to him.

"Yeah?"

"Thank you."

"You're welcome."

Night had set in, and the crickets were the only noise to greet Zac when he stepped outside the back door for a breath and a moment to calm down. Because all he could think about was all the things he didn't know about Sophie and all the things he yearned to discover. He was falling for her, fast, and if he wasn't careful, he'd risk not just his heart but Carrie's as well.

Once back inside, he grabbed the popcorn from the microwave, dumped it into a bowl, and handed it to Sophie.

"What's the movie?"

"*Jurassic World.*"

"Really?"

"Yeah, I never got a chance to see it. You look surprised."

"I just never would have pegged you for an action-movie girl. Thought for sure we'd be watching *Notting Hill* or some shit."

She laughed as she took a handful of popcorn, then passed the bowl to Zac. "Still a possibility if this one sucks."

"Nah, it's good. If you like action, you'll like it." He hit the lights, then settled back beside her as the movie came on. And it was a doozy. Sophie jumped at every turn, and before long, she set the popcorn bowl on the end table and pulled Zac closer to her so she could duck her head and hide her eyes every time a dinosaur jumped out.

Finally, Zac urged her to lie down, him behind her so her body was tucked up against his, his arms around her, holding her tightly to him. Then he felt something change. The movie continued to blast with the surround sound, but he was no longer paying attention. No, his focus was on her hand on his, gliding his hand down her thigh.

Then she turned slowly until she was lying flat on the couch, him still on his side. "You make me feel safe."

And then her free hand reached up and directed his face toward hers.

Their lips connected, and as though the simple touch had released something, she sighed against his lips. That tiny noise, barely vocalized, sent them into a frenzy. The kiss intensified, and Zac rolled on top of her, their bodies moving together, unable to remain still.

Zac's hands began to explore of their own accord, down her thigh, gripping her leg and wrapping it around his waist so he could cup her ass. She moaned this time, the sound so sweet that he nearly tore off her clothes right then and there, but he knew she needed to go slow.

So when she pulled back, he didn't follow. Instead, he brushed her hair from her face and stared down at her.

"I want to see your tattoos."

"My tattoos?"

"I know, it's stupid."

"It's not stupid." He pushed back onto his knees, then gripped his shirt and tugged it off, tossing it to the floor. Sophie sat up, and her eyes fixed on the compass over his right pectoral muscles. With a single finger, she traced the ink lines, then the claws over his shoulder that led to the tribal tattoo that wrapped around his back and down his arm.

"You're so perfect." Her eyes flicked up to his. "How can someone be so perfect?"

He stilled her hand over his heart. "I'm not a perfect person, Sophie. I make mistakes just like the rest of the world. But maybe, if you'll let me . . . I could be perfect for you."

He traced her lips, his gaze following the line, and then started in to kiss her again when his cell vibrated on the coffee table.

"Sorry, I have to . . ."

"Of course, make sure she's okay."

Grabbing his cell, Zac checked to see who had texted, only to find a message from Brooks asking if Zac was free for breakfast tomorrow. He set the phone back down and focused on Sophie.

"Is she okay?"

"It wasn't her. It was an old friend of mine, Brooks. He's coming back to town for a few days and wants to get together."

"I've heard his name. The only person to ever leave or something?"

"Yeah, he had some family problems. Left for college and never looked back. I'm a little surprised he's stopping by, but his parents are buried here, so he's probably . . ." Zac trailed off at the look on Sophie's face. "Or we could stop talking about this, and go back to . . ."

She sat up and kissed him lightly in answer. "I don't want you to sleep out here."

"No?"

"No."

An understanding passed between them, and Zac leaned over her, kissing her lips, then neck, his body hovering over her until she wrapped her arms around him and secured him to her. Their breaths came out in pants, the moment speeding up as the kiss built. Finally he couldn't take anymore.

Pushing off the couch, Zac scooped Sophie into his arms and started for the bedroom, a strange feeling passing over him with each step. Something that felt a lot like peace. As he set her gently on the edge of his king-size bed, not bothering to turn on the light, he decided he didn't want to rush this. No, this moment would remain in his memory for the rest of his life.

Without a word, him still in jeans and his chest bare, he reached down and traced the edge of her shirt, his fingertips gliding over her stomach. He eased it up and over her head, then tossed it to a nearby chair. His gaze dropped to her full breasts, barely contained within a light pink bra, nothing about it overly sexy, and yet . . .

He dropped to his knees before her, and she threaded her fingers into his hair, massaging his scalp—driving him insane.

"Sophie?"

"Yes." The response was less an answer and more a command.

He brushed her long, wavy hair from where it had fallen over her shoulder, then kissed the patch of freckles there, her collarbone, her neck, then the swell of her breasts, her body arching up to him, her head falling back, so eager.

And there went any chance of them going slow.

With one hand, he unfastened her bra, letting her breasts spill free, and holy hell. A man could die a very, very happy death before these breasts.

He lay her back and ran his hand down her stomach, then kissed her navel, before unsnapping her shorts and sliding them over her hips and to the floor. Her legs were shaking now, desire igniting every muscle in her body. Zac wanted to give her every pleasure that she deserved, fill every fantasy.

Trailing his fingertips gently down her thighs over her calves, he edged her legs open and pressed a kiss to the inside of her thigh, then one by one, he kissed every inch of her leg until she gripped his shoulders, her fingernails digging into his flesh, her need escalating to the point of pain. He knew it was time that he helped her find her release.

Slowly, he slipped her panties off. She squirmed on the bed, her hands tightening on his shoulders as he lowered his mouth to her mound, stroking the delicate flesh there with his tongue, before sucking her into his mouth, his tongue continuing its work, while he fought to keep himself from coming right there, her sweet taste all over him as she rose to his mouth, desperate to be claimed. And he was just the man to do it.

He licked her once more, then drove a finger deep inside her and sucked harder until she cried out, her body coiled tight. Then she collapsed back against the bed, her eyes still closed as she reached for him.

"I want you inside me," she breathed.

Zac took a condom from his nightstand and rolled it on, then stared down at this woman who'd come into his life like a tornado, tossing everything on its head, yet making everything better.

He bent over her and kissed her, then drove inside her while she wrapped her legs around his waist, drawing him still closer. They moved together, harder, faster, their eyes locked. Zac could swear that this, whatever it was, might destroy him. But damn if it wouldn't be the most satisfying breakdown of his life.

Sophie's eyes clenched tight, and he released in a surge of emotions, as if he could drop all the stress of his life for the first time and just breathe. Her hands in his, her eyes on his, her body wrapped around him. Through her, he could breathe again.

There were no sounds in the room as Zac pulled Sophie against him. No distractions, only the two of them—nothing fake about it.

His breathing slowed against her hair until they were both sound asleep.

Chapter Fourteen

"But why won't you tell me?" Glenda huffed as she followed Sophie into the Fresh Foods retail front. "You spent the night there. That has to mean frisky happenings, and I need to live vicariously through you. Please. Just one question."

"Fine, one." Sophie placed a hand on her hip, but she couldn't bring herself to be aggravated at her friend. In fact, nothing could upset her today. Not the neighbor's dog getting into her trash—again. Not the license check on her way to the farm, as though the sheriff didn't know every single person in Crestler's Key without having to look at his or her ID. And then she arrived at the farm to find the lock had been broken off the main gate—likely an accident rather than anything serious. Just yesterday, she would have been worried about such a thing, but after spending the night in Zac's arms, him giving her satisfaction in more ways than one—more times than she could count—she decided life was too short to worry about things that were very likely in her head.

So someone called and hung up a few times.

So someone sent her wildflowers.

So the lock on the gate had been broken.

Each thing could have a very logical explanation, and Sophie refused to search out problems that weren't there.

"Okay," Glenda said, rubbing her hands together in excitement. "How big is his—"

"No way. Not going there."

"What? I was going to say tattoo. Get your mind out of the gutter. But of course, if you decide you want to dish on the other, then I'm all ears."

Sophie rolled her eyes and flicked on the lights. "What makes you think I know the answer to either of those questions?"

Of course she did, and the answer was big. Like *big* big. On both accounts.

She giggled at the thought, and Glenda pointed at her. "That's what. You can't stop smiling, and you're laughing like a fool. That reaction only happens when you have really great sex or you fall in love. So which is it?" Sophie stopped walking, and Glenda's excitement soared to the sky. "Oh my God. You love him."

"What? No. I barely know him."

"Of course you know him. You've lived here for like six months or whatever, right? And you two have been dating for nearly a month now. You could totally love him."

"But I don't." Not yet. Though Sophie felt she could love him. Zac represented everything she'd always wanted in a man but never considered for herself. He was a family man, loyal to the core, strong and dependable. And it didn't hurt that in one night he'd awoken some sort of sexual fiend inside of her, all too eager to explore every inch of his body.

"Sophie."

She glanced over to find Glenda barely containing her laughter.

"You overfilled the flowerpot."

Sophie focused on the water pitcher in her hand, which she didn't even remember picking up, and then the overflowing pot of tulips. "Craptastic." Jumping back, she set the pitcher down and grabbed a fresh towel from the back to clean up the spill.

"Maybe not love, but you like him."

Sophie stopped what she was doing and leaned back on her heels, grinning up at her friend. "I do. I so do. Is that terrible though? I mean he's a father. Surely there are rules against that kind of thing."

"So what? Carrie-Anne is adorable, and you aren't the kind of woman to try to put a wedge between them."

"Lord no. I'm the opposite, actually. I want them to stay exactly as they are. Just . . . let me spend a little time with them in the mix." She stared out the floor-length windows that looked out over the farm, then back at Glenda, who had her hands linked in front of her and was shaking her head slowly. "What?"

"Nothing. I'm just so happy for you. Since you moved here you've sort of looked like a fish out of water, trying to find your way, but not quite getting there. You were always the sweet person you are, but it never touched your eyes. Not like now. You look very happy."

"I am. He's just . . . amazing. I'm so going to screw it up. But until then, I plan to hold on for dear life."

The two women laughed at the same time that Kit, their UPS driver, arrived with some packages. "Here you go, Sophie. Same place as always?"

She waved a hello. "Yep, on the counter is fine, and I have a little treat for you there to give Abby."

He set down the packages and returned with the jar of honey she'd fixed up for him. "You shouldn't have."

"Tell her to mix a little with green tea, and it'll help that sore throat she's been having."

"Thanks. I'll tell her. You ladies have anything for me?"

"Not today, but we'll have a mess of shipments for you to-morrow."

"Sounds good."

They waved him off, and Glenda went to work opening the pack-ages before stopping at one. "Hey, this one's addressed to you, not Fresh Foods."

Sophie pushed off the floor and tossed the towel onto the counter, then eyed the package. "Weird. Maybe it's samples from a supplier or something."

"Maybe. Open it."

Shrugging, Sophie grabbed a pair of scissors from the basket of miscellaneous items she kept beside the register and slit open the box, only to cut her hand in the process. "Yikes." She stared down at the cut and pressed it to her mouth as Nana had taught her to do to stop the bleeding. But today the bleeding chose not to listen.

"I'll grab you a Band-Aid. Stay put."

"Thanks." With her good hand, she tore open the rest of the pack-age to find a bubble-wrapped figure inside. Slowly, she worked the wrapping off the figure and then stared down at the angel, her left wing broken. In an instant she was back there.

They'd gone out to dinner on Sophie's birthday, and the restau-rant had served her a sundae in honor of her special day. He didn't like her to eat desserts, and she'd gotten in the habit of politely refus-ing them at birthday parties and weddings, always saying she was full and couldn't eat another bite. But the restaurant owner had come out and was adamant that she enjoy his treat for her.

So she did.

Somehow she went from taking a small bite that wouldn't impact her waistline to inhaling the entire bowl. She would have been embarrassed if not for the owner's excitement, but then her eyes had lifted to find him watching her, a look of pure disgust on his face.

When they arrived home, he sat her down in the family room and explained what she'd done, how detrimental it was to her health and his because he needed her in top shape for his work functions, and what would his colleagues think if he were married to an obese wife. She listened to each word, each painful slice to her self-esteem, and then she apologized, sure that was the end of it. It always had been before. But then he stood and reached for her hand. She had no idea what he was doing when he led her to the bathroom, turned on the light, and flipped up the lid on the toilet seat.

"It's your only option now," he'd said. Then he placed the small angel beside her and closed the door.

That was the first time of many that she would purge herself of all the bad foods she'd eaten, each time with the angel beside her.

Until finally, one beautiful fall day, she snapped.

He placed the angel on the sink, and Sophie stared down at it, this petite, beautiful little angel, nothing but love on the angel's face. Sophie picked it up, opened the bathroom door, and threw it as hard as she could.

She packed her bags that day, him belittling her the entire time, but he never hurt her. No, his idea of pain wasn't inflicted by actions, but by words. By a constant, unyielding tick at her self-worth until there was nothing left.

And now he'd found her.

The phone calls, the flowers, the gate—they weren't random. They weren't kids joking around, customers offering their kindness, accidents. They were him.

"Here you go." Glenda placed the Band-Aid on the counter, then took the angel from her. "What is it?"

"A gift."

"From who?"

Sophie lifted her chin and stared out the windows over the farm and the life she'd created. "My husband."

* * *

Zac arrived early at Brighton's for breakfast with Brooks the next morning, his body still humming from a night that he would never forget.

Dangerous thoughts circled through his head, thoughts about a future, about dinners around the kitchen table filled with laughter. About not having to have the dreaded dating talk with Carrie because maybe there would be someone better to have it.

"Want some coffee, hun?" Lindy asked, her cropped hair as red as ever.

"Coffee sounds great, thanks."

She took the cup from in front of him and filled it. Zac took a long sip, his second cup of the day—the first shared in bed with Sophie hours before.

"Whoa, didn't know you were capable of smiling that big."

Zac glanced up and then pushed out of his chair, excitement pouring out of him as he clapped hands with his old friend. "Dude, I didn't even see you walk up. How goes it?"

"Clearly not as good as you," Brooks said. "Some lady in your life these days producing that smile, or is business just that good?"

"Hey, I'm not the real estate mogul. Rumor has it you swim around in money like Scrooge McDuck."

Brooks laughed, never one to brag about his wealth. Maybe because growing up he never had any. But since leaving Crestler's Key and going to college, he'd bought homes cheap, fixed them up, and then rented them out. Which might seem like small fish, but in time, he'd made a fortune and opened up a real shop for various real estate investments, even buying things for other people and taking a cut of the profit. He was smart on a ridiculous level, so it shouldn't have surprised Zac that he'd done so well.

"Ah, I do okay. But let's get back to you looking like you just scored the winning home run. What's up with you these days? How's Carrie?"

Zac had seen Brooks only a handful of times over the years, so he filled him in on Carrie, the farm, Southern Dive, and then finally he landed on Sophie.

"Sounds serious," Brooks said as he took a sip of his coffee and started in on the pancakes he'd ordered.

"I don't know. She moved here to help her grandmother who—

hey, come to think of it. Didn't you work for her grandmother, Gwendolyn? Wasn't that one of the lawns you covered?"

"Hard to say. I mowed a lot of lawns back then, all for shit money."

Zac laughed. "I remember."

"But you like her."

Zac thought back to last night, how desperate he'd been to hold on to her for just a few more minutes this morning. "Yeah . . . I do."

"Think she's the one?"

Zac stared around Brighton's Sandwich Shop, half the town's ears pricked for information that he wasn't ready to share.

"I don't know about that."

"That's she's the one?"

"I don't know if I believe in the sentiment. I think love is something you work on, day in and day out. I don't think calling someone 'the one' gets you out of that work. If anything, you have to work harder to keep it going."

Yet even as he said it, Zac thought it didn't feel like work with Sophie, and he suspected it never would. Having his wife walk out on their family had left him with jaded thoughts on things like dating and women and the ideals of forever. But maybe those ideals weren't a fantasy after all.

"Seems a little fast if you ask me."

Zac's gaze snapped back to Brooks, someone he hadn't seen in six months, who was here now to what? Pass judgment on his relationship? "What's that supposed to mean?"

"Nothing. I just don't want to see you get hurt again. I mean, what do you really know about her? Has she been married before, like you have?"

"No, never married."

"Never married. Seriously? Seems a little odd, don't you think? That a woman like her wouldn't have been married before?"

The sandwich shop had become hot all of a sudden, a tendril of doubt swirling in Zac's stomach. "She said she's never been married."

"And you believe her?"

"Why wouldn't I?"

Brooks popped a slice of bacon in his mouth and shrugged. "Just wondering how much you know about her is all. Ignore me."

But Zac couldn't. Because the truth was, he didn't know much about her. He knew she'd been with someone who'd hurt her in some way, that she'd left Merryville to move here to help her grandmother. Though come to think of it, Sophie had never told him that bit. He'd surmised it from the various conversations he'd had with her and rumors he'd heard since she arrived. And then she bought the farm, but she'd explained that part to him, and it wasn't like it mattered if she bought a farm. That didn't affect him having a relationship with her.

But her being married and lying about it?

Zac tried to put it out of his mind, telling himself that it wasn't an issue. He and Sophie had talked about their relationships. Only, they hadn't exactly. But what did that matter? They didn't need to know every sordid detail of each other's past to be together. Did they? No. This was just getting started. It was—

"Hey, seriously. Ignore me. You look like you're getting freaked out."

"I'm fine. Enough about me. Tell me what's been going on with you."

And then Zac tried to listen as Brooks dove into business ventures, travelling, everything in his life, before finally saying, "I'm actually thinking about staying here for a while."

"In Crestler's Key? Really?"

"Yeah." He took a bite of his toast, then a long sip of his water. "Nice to be back home."

"Sounds like we'll get to see if you can still throw a fastball then."

Brooks laughed and leaned back in his chair. "Name the day, brother, and I'm game. I'm not going anywhere anytime soon."

Chapter Fifteen

"Okay, so I know I said I wouldn't ask, but I have to ask," Glenda said.

It'd been hours since she'd revealed that she was still married, though the still-being-married part was not for lack of trying. Her legal separation had been signed, and the divorce had been filed but it wasn't finalized yet. He had refused to sign and then contested the divorce on grounds, a thought that made Sophie's stomach twist into a pretzel.

She drew a breath. "I'm separated, but technically I'm still married."

"And you think your husband sent the angel."

Sophie turned around to face the apple pie she'd just pulled from the oven. "I know he did." Then Sophie did the last thing she thought she'd ever do—she told someone. Everything.

She opened up about their early days, how kind he'd been, how handsome, how sure she'd been that they'd spend forever together. And then how each success he had at work seemed to make him grow colder to her until she felt like another piece of his company, something for him to shape and mold into the perfect wife, the perfect accessory. Only she would never be perfect enough.

As Sophie wrapped up her story, Glenda sat down and shook her head. "I'm so sorry. If I'd known . . . I'm sorry." Then she stood up, walked over, and placed a hand on Sophie's. "Maybe you should stay with me for a couple of days. Just until this is sorted out. I mean, if you think he's here."

"I don't know. This could just mean he's agreeing to the divorce and the rest is in my head."

"But what if it's not? Does Zac know?"

"No. And you can't tell him. We're just becoming something, and he's already untrusting of women."

"This isn't your fault, though. Surely he would understand."

"He asked me if I was married. I told him no."

"That's not a lie. You're not technically, and that jerk of a husband of yours doesn't deserve to call you his wife any longer. Zac would understand. You want him to trust you, so trust him back. Tell him the truth—all of it."

Sophie put in a call to her lawyer after she left the farm. Just to be safe. But he assured her that they'd filed for a restraining order and everything had been documented. The divorce would be finalized soon, despite Mark contesting the grounds, and she could finally put it all behind her.

"And the restraining order is still active, right?" Sophie's breath felt heavy in her chest, her fears climbing higher and higher, making it difficult to stand.

"It's intact. He can't come within a hundred yards of you."

She drew a long, rattled breath and thought of the broken lock again. "And what if he does?"

"Then you call the cops, and he'll get arrested." Pat paused, and Sophie heard a door close on his end of the line. "How is therapy going?"

"Good, I guess. I mean, I stopped going really, but I call when I need to."

"Has something happened? Is there something else going on that I should know about? If he's contacted you . . ."

Sophie hesitated, her gaze drifting out to the main gate. "I don't know. There's just a few things . . . it's probably nothing."

"Not with a man like Mark. If something has you worried, you need to tell me."

"It's probably nothing," Sophie repeated.

"Sophie. Tell me."

"Fine." She unloaded each of the instances that concerned her, finishing with the angel, which still had Sophie shaking. "It could be his way of saying he signed the papers."

"I don't think so. He's still contesting."

"So you think . . ."

"It's hard to say, but I'm going to call the local law enforcement to let them know what's going on so they can watch out for him. I'll send a photo. It's probably nothing, as you said, but we can't be too careful."

"I don't think he would hurt me."

"But Sophie, he already has. Not all injuries are visible to the eye. You know this."

She nodded, though Pat couldn't see her. "Right. I know you're right."

"I'll call and send the photo, and you call my cell if you need anything at all, okay?"

Her lips trembled, her right leg jumping in time, her whole body succumbing to fear. Again. How could he weasel his way back into her mind so easily?

"Okay, thanks."

Hanging up, she scrolled through her contacts until she found Zac's number and hit Call just so she could hear his voice and feel a bit of the reassurance and comfort he provided. So she could forget all the rest for a few precious moments.

"Just who I was talking about. How are you?"

"Better now," she admitted.

"I want to see you."

"Now?"

"I wish, but I'm stuck at the farm for a few more minutes. Deliveries today."

"I know the feeling."

"But my friend Brooks wanted to meet you. Are you up for an early dinner? Say in half an hour? Captain Jack's?"

"Sounds great. How was Brooks?"

"Really good. He's thinking of moving back here actually."

"That's great news. I look forward to meeting him."

"So five thirty?"

She closed her eyes, taking in Zac's deep voice, a promise of protection laced within it. "I'll be there."

Sophie closed herself in her Mini Cooper, checked the back seat, and locked the doors, then did each again for good measure. Talking with Zac had calmed her a bit, but she needed to figure out what was going on with Mark if she ever hoped to feel one hundred percent safe. And deep down she knew there was only one thing she could do to end this for good—she would have to face him. Until this point, she'd had everything go through her lawyer. She gave up the house and all assets. She didn't want anything from him, so it should have been easy. But Mark was well connected and had some of the best lawyers out there, so it shouldn't have surprised her that he contested the divorce on grounds, demanding she prove that he was abusive. Something hard to do when he'd never once put a hand on her.

For months, Sophie fought and fought, giving her lawyer everything she could to fight him, but finally she grew tired and told her lawyer she needed a break. Pat couldn't understand why Mark wouldn't simply agree to the divorce, but he didn't understand that Sophie was keeping the one asset Mark valued most—her.

The town was quiet for late afternoon, most people still at work closing up their days, so Sophie wasn't surprised to find Captain Jack's parking lot nearly empty when she arrived. In a few hours, it would be packed. But for now, she could walk out on the back deck and down the dock, looking over the water without a crowd around to watch her.

She locked her car, then went inside, waving a hello to Jack.

"Table today?"

"Yes, we have three today, but Zac and his friend aren't here yet. Is it okay if I walk outside before he gets here?"

"Help yourself. Want a drink for the journey?"

"Thanks, that'd be great. Sweet tea?"

"Coming up."

A few tables were full of older folks who enjoyed eating early, regulars who were often here each night. Sophie waved a hello to them, and while most stared at her like she was crazy, a few waved back. Zac's influence, no doubt, but she would take it.

"Here you go, dear. Give me a yell if you need anything. I'll have Trixie set up a table for you by the windows."

"Perfect. Thanks."

She walked outside and down the sloping dock to the end and sat down, her legs hanging over the side, and thought about what Glenda had said about telling Zac. Maybe he would understand. Maybe he could even offer some advice. Maybe he would hug her close and say they'd work it out.

Or maybe he would walk away.

The thought hurt her heart so badly that she pressed her palm to her chest in hopes of soothing the ache. She'd been hurt before, her mind and heart torn in two, but Zac had given her hope that she could have a normal life again. A life with him. Why hadn't she just told him the truth?

Maybe because the thought of talking about Mark made her want to curl into a ball. If she said she'd been married, then she would have been forced to talk about her husband, and he didn't get to be a part of her world now. He didn't deserve that.

"There you are."

Warmth flooded Sophie's chest, and a smile stretched across her face. She stood up and turned around, eager to see the man who'd broken through her fears.

Then everything in her world came to a screeching halt.

Instead of her eyes landing on Zac, they'd locked on the man standing beside him, a knowing grin on his face, and suddenly she couldn't breathe.

"I'm from a small town," he'd said. *"Middle of nowhere, Kentucky."*

No.

"I used to play baseball. Third base like Brooks Robinson."

No, no, no.

Sophie tried to breathe, tried to tell her body to remember how to work properly, but all the blood had drained from her head, and stars dotted the corners of her vision, everything going dark as her heart sped up.

"What are you doing here? You can't be here."

Zac started for her. "Dinner, remember? Are you . . . ?" He trailed off as his gaze drifted from Sophie to the man beside him and back. "You weren't talking to me, were you?'

"Sophie, it's time for you to come home."

"Can someone tell me what the hell is going on here?" The look on Zac's face would have brought Sophie back if only she could focus on him. But she couldn't.

Because standing beside the man who had lifted her from the grave was the man who'd put her there.

Chapter Sixteen

"Someone explain what the hell is going on. Now."

Zac couldn't shake the feeling that he was about to play the fool for the second time in his adult life. He wanted to walk back inside and come back out in hopes of finding a different situation before him. He should leave, now, before whatever this was exploded in his face. But he couldn't stop looking at Sophie, glancing both ways on the dock, water all around her, her hands out, a look of unadulterated fear on her face.

"I'm sorry, Zac," Brooks said. "I haven't been fully honest with you. Nor has my wife."

"Wife?" Ice crept through Zac's veins, over his heart, anger replacing the care he'd felt just moments before.

He took a step toward Sophie, then stopped, his feet no longer able to move. "You said you weren't married. You said . . ." He glanced from Brooks to Sophie, sure he'd stumbled into an alternate universe. Never once had Brooks mentioned being married in all the times they'd talked over the years. Never once.

Brooks took a step toward Sophie, and she jerked away. "Please. Just stop." He took another step, and Zac thought Sophie was going to jump into the water. "Stop."

Then he remembered her talk about her last relationship, the fear on her face when she spoke of it, how badly she had been shaking when she came to his house after the flower delivery. And despite the confusion of the situation, a greater part of him said he needed to help her now.

Taking a step around Brooks, he eased him back, Zac a good three inches taller than him with thirty extra pounds of muscle. "I don't know what's going on here, but I do know that a woman shouldn't be that afraid of the person who's claiming to be her husband."

"She's insane. That's why I came here. To get her some help."

Now all of Captain Jack's back windows were full of people watching. Half the town would have gotten texts by now, likely with photos attached—check out the love triangle! What was he thinking, risking Carrie-Anne like this? Exposing her to town gossip that he would have to explain, her once again caught in the middle.

He needed Sophie to say something, to deny Brooks's claim, so he could fix this in his mind before he completely shut down.

Turning slowly, he prepared to ask Sophie for the truth, to explain, but in the time it'd taken Zac to stop Brooks from going to her, she'd disappeared.

He spun around in time to find Brooks rushing back toward the restaurant. Zac grabbed him and threw him back. "You. Explain. Now."

Brooks straightened his shirt and glared at Zac. "I don't have to explain anything to you. Sophie's my wife. That's the only explanation you need to stay the hell away from her."

Zac focused back on the water, none of this working in his mind. "How come you never mentioned her? Or even that you were married?"

He shrugged. "It never came up."

"You being married never came up."

"I'm a private person."

"A wife isn't something you keep a secret. What's really going on here? What aren't you saying, and why is she so scared?"

"How am I supposed to know? Probably because she was caught. Think about your wife, Zac. How did she look when you caught her in the act?" Then Brooks shook his head, a flash of hurt on his face. "I never thought you, of all people, would become the other man."

That cut deep, and Zac wanted to walk away so badly he had to force his legs to remain still. "I mentioned your name to her. She didn't react. Not even a little bit. She would have said something, reacted in some way, if she knew someone named Brooks."

"That's because she and most everyone else in my life call me by my real name."

Zac closed his eyes. "Mark." He had called Brooks by the nickname since they'd played Little League together, a bunch of eight-year-olds who thought they were bigger than they were. Mark was a natural at third, so they started calling him Brooks after Brooks Robinson, and the name stuck.

"So you . . ."

"We've been married for three years."

The world was spinning now, and though Zac wanted to trust Sophie, believe in the person she'd been to him, he couldn't argue with Brooks's story. Sophie had hidden so much of herself. Was this the reason? That she'd left her husband behind?

Zac felt sick to the core. Unable to handle any more with the town as audience, he walked away, out of Captain Jack's and away from yet another heartbreak. Now twice in his life he'd been lied to, been the fool.

Well, no more. He was done.

Sophie couldn't stop shaking. On the dash to her car, the entire ride home. Every second she glanced in her rearview mirror, and at every stop she double-checked that her car was locked. He was here. He had found her.

Now what would he do to her?

The thought caused her hands to shake so violently that she struggled to grip the steering wheel. She needed to get out of here, pack a bag, and disappear.

But then he would just track her down again, and she couldn't hide forever. She would have to face him.

So when she drove down her drive and found a mysterious Jeep Wrangler parked outside her house, she fought the urge to turn back, to run and run and run, and instead drew a long breath. She quickly sent a text to Glenda, telling her to come check on her if she didn't hear from her in twenty minutes, and stepped out of her car.

Mark was sitting on her front porch in her rocking chair, her cat in his lap, which meant he'd been in her house. A shudder, which she tried to ignore, worked through her. Had he broken into her house before? Had he watched her while she was sleeping?

"The restraining order says you can't be here."

He cocked a perfect blond head, steel gray eyes burrowing into her like they knew every one of her secrets, her fears. "My team said that wasn't binding while we're contesting. That I can go wherever I like."

Sophie wasn't sure if he was lying. He spoke a lie as easily as the truth, one switched out for the other whenever he liked. "Fine. Then you won't mind my calling the police."

"Tell Tom I said hello."

Her blood turned to ice. "I don't want anything from you. Why can't you leave me alone?"

He placed her cat down on the front porch, then stood, the rocking chair whining as it rocked back. He took the two steps down to the front yard and started slowly for her. "But see, therein lies the problem. You think what you want matters here, and it doesn't. I want something from you. And I get what I want. Always."

Sophie took a step back, and he matched it forward. "What do you want?"

He tilted his chin up and fixed her with the stare that had filled her nightmares for months after she left.

"I never told you this, but I knew your grandmother. Quite well. Gwendolyn hired me to mow her grass and trim her bushes when I was barely ten years old. She'd invite me inside after I was done and give me milk and cookies. My mother never made cookies. So I would mow Gwendolyn's grass, then eat her cookies, and then I'd listen to her talk about her perfect granddaughter. With her long blond hair and blue eyes, beautiful and perfect in every way."

"You knew me."

"I listened to every story Gwendolyn ever told about you, each time gaining more information, more reasons why you needed to be mine. And then Gwendolyn slipped. It was an accident of course. She had no idea of my affections when she left out a birthday card from you to her. And finally, I had your address."

"But look at you, you could have had anyone. Why me?"

"Because she loved you, and I loved her."

Sophie felt her body go numb. She searched her memories for any mention of Mark, but there was nothing. Nana never—

Wait. The sweet blond boy. Nana had never mentioned him to Sophie when she was well, but she'd talked of him at the nursing home, talked about how his parents ignored him, how she worried there was abuse. The blond boy must have been Mark.

He edged closer to her, and she took another step back, her eyes locked on his, which kept drifting down and back up her body.

"Please, just tell me what you want."

"You."

Chapter Seventeen

Zac grabbed a beer from his fridge, grateful that his daughter wasn't home to see him wallowing in his misery. He wanted to call Sophie, he wanted to ask her to explain everything, but he couldn't bring himself to hear what she might say—that Brooks had told the truth. They were married, and Zac had helped her commit adultery.

The thought wreaked havoc on Zac's insides. He contemplated calling his mom to ask her to pick up Carrie from school so he could get out of town for a few hours and think. But he wasn't the sort of man who ran from things, and besides, this was his home—his town—not hers. If someone needed to leave, it was her.

He'd just decided to turn his sadness to anger when his doorbell rang. Immediately, he went still, praying that if he didn't make a sound, the person—likely one of his brothers—would go away. But instead, the doorbell was followed by knocking, and then a loud female voice called, "Open up. Please."

With a long sigh, Zac pushed to standing and walked to the door, opening it only enough to see Glenda on the other side, her expression frantic. "Is Sophie here?"

"Why would she be here? She's probably with her *husband*." He took a long pull of his beer.

Glenda pushed open the door and stormed in. "God, I had no idea you were such an idiot."

"Thanks."

"He isn't her husband. At least not legally."

"Wait, what did you say?" That had his attention.

"They're legally separated. She has a restraining order against him. She's filed for divorce, but he refuses to sign. Contested the grounds."

"Restraining order?"

"He's dangerous, Zac."

"Shit."

"Wait, where are you going?"

"Where I should have gone from the beginning—to Sophie's."

Sophie felt like her legs had turned to jelly, and her hands refused to stop shaking. But her brain was solid. Her mind focused on the man across from her, inching her way, his intentions perfectly clear.

He had come to Crestler's Key for her, and he had no intention of leaving without her.

A surge of worry burst through Sophie's gut, but for once she refused to succumb to it. In ten more minutes, Glenda would be here if Sophie didn't call, so Sophie had ten minutes to convince a maniac that he should leave, now, and never bother her again. And if she couldn't, then Glenda would come—with the police, Sophie hoped.

But a lot could happen in ten minutes, and suddenly Sophie's desire to flee overwhelmed her.

The thing about a man like Mark, though—he wouldn't give up unless he made the decision to end this, not her. To really be free of him, she needed to convince him that she was beneath him. That she couldn't be rebuilt. That she, Sophie Marsh, was a waste of time and effort.

Just the thought made her body quake like an injured animal hiding from a predator, a silent plea for mercy. But Sophie would never feel safe unless she were truly free from him.

"But here's the thing. You don't want me. Not really."

"And what would you know about what I want?" He paused midstep, and Sophie took the opportunity to edge back a few inches, no more, but every inch felt like an inch toward her freedom.

"Plenty. I listened to you work deals. I watched your reactions when you took on a new client, purchased new real estate. I prepared dinners for your staff, attended countless parties. I know your standards. And I know with certainty that I will never reach them."

His gaze locked on hers, his brain churning, and she knew if she had any chance, it was now. With every bit of the strength of a woman who would no longer live in fear, she took a step toward him.

"Honestly, it's hard for me to admit it, to know that I'm never going to be enough. It's why I had to leave. Not for me . . . but for you."

He lifted his chin. "You left for me."

"I wasn't lying when I said our vows. That love, my feelings, they were—are—real for me. And if I've learned anything from watching you, it's that you know when to put someone out of his or her misery. You fire them before they fire themselves. You save them from themselves. I had to do the same for you. Because me? I'll never be on your level."

Another step.

"You're brilliant, top of your class. You created a multimillion dollar business in your free time while getting your MBA. Me? I've never accomplished anything in my life. And I'm trying now, I am. But even if I work for the rest of my life, I will never reach your potential."

Another step, this one so close that she could see the lines around his eyes as he squinted in the sun, watching her, listening to her.

"And then there's the physical differences. You . . ." She stared adoringly at him while her insides screamed for her to stop lying, to punch him like he deserved. Still, she pushed on.

"You're perfect. Your hair, your eyes, your body." She let her eyes scan down him as though it were hard for her to look away. "You're the example of what to strive for. And me? My body is every woman's worst nightmare, and my face . . ." Her lip trembled, and she looked away. "Look, I know I'm not very pretty. I know that I was lucky to be with you, lucky that you took pity on a girl like me and gave me a chance. But I've watched the women in our circle stare at you for too long. I've listened as waitresses half our age threw themselves at you. And I've tried to ignore it, tried to put aside my jealousy for you, but one day it hit me—I can't be what you need me to be. I will never be what you need me to be."

Sophie was to him now, her hand outstretched to cradle his cheek, the gesture so against her instincts that she had to force herself not to flinch.

"I'm not asking you to let me leave. I'm asking you to save yourself. You deserve more."

Mark drew a long breath, his gaze still on hers, and then he nodded slowly. "You're right." He placed his hand over hers.

Sophie started to exhale for the first time until his hand tightened and his eyes narrowed.

"I am better than you. In every way. But the heart wants what it wants." He twisted her arm behind her, securing her to him, tightening his hold on her arm until she screamed.

"Did you scream while Zac was inside you? Did you call his name?" He wrenched her forearm until blinding pain sliced through her, her vision blurring as she tried to breathe, to fight against him, only to have him strengthen his hold.

"You will pay for your betrayal, and when you're done, you will make me forget that he ever had you. You will show me again and again and again that I'm the only man who gets this." His free hand slipped down her body, and something inside her snapped.

Because everything she said to Mark was correct. She wasn't as intelligent as him. But she was a quick learner. She wasn't as successful as him. But she was driven. She wasn't as beautiful as him. But her heart was kind.

And finally Sophie understood that these things weren't weaknesses. They were strengths. They were reminders that she was unique and beautiful in her own way. And Zac saw that, too. He pulled her close and made her feel special. Because to him, she was special.

To herself she was special, and she owed it to herself to fight.

So when Sophie let her body go slack in Mark's arms and he let up for a fraction of a second, he wasn't prepared for her to stomp on his foot and then elbow him in the gut and take off running. Her arm throbbed, and her shoulder was likely dislocated, but she couldn't deal with that now. Right now she had to run, she had to make it to her car, she had to—

An arm wrapped around her waist, and then they were on the ground, her clawing in the dirt to get away as Mark gripped her hips and spun her around, his expression maniacal.

"You're rougher now. We'll need to work that out of you."

"Work this out." And then she spit in his face, only to have him rear back and slap her across the face so hard she saw stars, her skin smarting, her eye throbbing from the impact. It was the first time he'd ever hit her, but instead of crying from the pain, she let a smile tip her lips. Because now, he'd done the one thing his lawyers claimed he'd never done—he'd hit her.

Before she could help herself, she started laughing, the sound bubbling up from deep inside her, refusing to be ignored. "Thank you."

"What did you say?"

"I said thank you. You just guaranteed that our divorce will be finalized."

Realization crossed his face, followed immediately by blood-curdling rage. He growled as he edged toward her, his teeth gritted together. She saw in his eyes that he'd crossed over to the other side. He would make her pay in ways she could only imagine. For the first time, Sophie thought she might not survive this day. Panic surged through her as she struggled against his hold, her shoulder burning in pain.

"Mark, please . . ."

"Say it again."

Her bottom lip trembled. "Please."

He cocked his head, and then a wicked smile split his face. He opened his mouth to speak, but instead, the sharp click of metal filled the air, followed by another voice, a voice so intense it almost sounded like a different person.

"Step off. Now."

Tears burned Sophie's eyes as she turned toward the voice. Zac stood several feet away, a nine millimeter raised, an expression on his face that said he was more than trained to use it.

Mark stood slowly, his hands outstretched. "What are you doing, man? You know me."

"Do I?" Zac asked, taking a step closer and then another. "Because I don't think I do. But you *do* know me, and you know that if you take a step toward her, I will end you right here and now."

"Zac, this is all a misunderstanding. Let me—" He started to lower his hands.

Sophie pushed herself to standing and backed away as Zac called out, "I don't want to shoot you, but I will."

Mark's hands went back up, and then several blue lights sped down Sophie's driveway. Sophie closed her eyes, relief pouring over her as she slumped to the ground. She drew a much-needed breath.

The sounds of police officer voices, Miranda rights being read, and then a familiar woodsy scent washing over her were the last things she remembered before everything went dark.

Chapter Eighteen

Zac stared down at the woman who'd taken over his world, an IV in her left arm, her right bandaged after being popped into place, and a fresh wave of guilt worked through him. What was he thinking? Why did he trust someone from his past who he rarely saw over Sophie? Why didn't he go to her, ask her to explain?

Because he was afraid, and he let that fear dictate his actions. And that single bad decision could have cost him the love of his life. The more he thought about it, the more he knew it was true—he loved her. Loved every single thing about her, and it was his job to protect her. He had promised her he would . . . and he failed her.

He ran his hands through his hair and closed his eyes, threading his fingertips together. "I'm sorry. I'm so damn sorry."

"It's not your fault."

His eyes snapped open, and he jumped up. "You're awake."

Sophie grimaced as she shifted in her hospital bed. "I'm starting to wish I wasn't, though."

"Dislocated shoulder. They put it back in place but said it would be sore for a while. I can go get your nurse. Ask her to give you more drugs or something." He started to walk away.

Sophie reached out for him, then grimaced again. "Please don't go."

The look of terror on her face made him wish he could trade places with her, his shoulder for hers, his pain for her relief. But this wasn't about him, and he refused to let his guilt make it about him. Instead, he walked back over and sat on the side of her bed, then took her hand in his. "I'm not going anywhere."

She released a breath and then her eyes filled with tears. Zac held her close as she cried against his chest, all the tension pouring out of her with each drop of emotion.

Finally, her tears dried up, and Zac took a tissue from the box beside her bed, blotted her eyes, and smoothed back her hair.

"I should have told you. If I'd told you, none of this would have happened."

"You don't know that. You were scared. I get how fear can define you. But you don't have to be scared anymore. I'm here. And I'm not going anywhere. I'm so sorry I didn't go straight to your house from Captain Jack's. I'm sorry I didn't let you explain while I listened with an open mind. I'm sorry I didn't deck Mark the moment I saw the fear on your face. I'm sorry I didn't tell you that I loved you last night. Because I do. I knew it then, but I didn't say anything because we're not ready for that. You're not ready for that. But I do love you. More than I thought it was possible for me to love another person again, and I'm willing to do whatever it takes to prove to you that my love is here, waiting for you. When and if you ever want to accept it."

"You love me?"

"So much it hurts."

Sophie took his hand and stared into Zac's eyes. "I love you, too. I'm nervous, and I don't know how to make these feelings work in my head right now, but I do. I know I do." Sophie closed her eyes and sighed, the first hint of contentment crossing her face. "I'm so tired. So, so tired. But I'm afraid to sleep. Will you lie with me? Just until I fall asleep?"

Zac traced her cheek and gently kissed her forehead before settling in beside her, careful not to agitate her shoulder. "I'll lie with you as long as you need."

She closed her eyes again.

"Thank you for loving me."

"Thank you for being you."

Sophie settled against him and smiled once more, before drifting off to peaceful sleep.

Epilogue

"What do you mean I have to get in line?" Sophie tapped her gel nails against the table, Fire Captain Justin before her, blocking her from view.

"Well, we just didn't think it would be fair if you got to bid on Zac first. You're a sponsor, and you supplied all the baskets this year for the auction, and the Littleton brothers are always a big hit. So we decided . . ."

Sophie pushed her hair back behind her shoulders and stood taller so Mr. Six Foot a Gagillion Inches would know that she might be small, but she would lower his ass if he didn't get out of her way and let her bid on her man.

Annie-Jean took the stage again, and Sam Hunt blared out over the speakers. "Next up we have our very own homegrown, deliciously handy, and perfectly tattooed Zac Littleton."

Sophie tried to edge around Justin, but he held her back while the bidding started, and Sophie saw red. One by one, women raised their little fans, bidding again and again, higher and higher, oblivious to the fact that Zac was taken—120 percent taken. They couldn't have him, not even for a good cause like the fire department. And besides, if Justin didn't get the hell out of her way, this whole event was going to be a waste because Sophie's head would explode and burn down the whole thing.

"He's going to think I don't care. I have to bid."

"He knows we're holding you back."

"What?" Sophie shouted.

A woman from the back jumped the bidding by a hundred dollars, and Sophie had had enough.

She acted as though she were going to go left, then she jumped right and ran around Justin, narrowly escaping his outstretched hands.

"Going once, going twice," Annie-Jean said.

"One thousand dollars," Sophie said as she rushed toward the stage. But she hadn't counted on the floor being so slippery and her heels being so wobbly, so she began to windmill in an effort to stop herself, but there was no stopping now. She tumbled headfirst to the floor.

A slow, entirely too sexy grin spread across Zac's face at the same time that Annie-Jean called, "Sold to Sophie Marsh. Who might be injured now, so if she is, last bidder wins."

Zac hopped off the stage and made his way to Sophie, his voice tinged with enthusiasm as he asked, "Need a hand there, sweetheart, or are you searching for something down there?"

Sophie glared at him as she stood up and brushed off her skirt, adjusted her hair, then stared at the man she loved. "You told Justin he could hold me back?"

"No, I told him I didn't want to do this in the first place, but you said I had to. So here I am."

"He made me wait to bid."

"He baited you."

"He what? Oh, I'll show him bait." Sophie spun around to go off on Justin, but Zac wrapped a hand around her middle instead.

"I'm sure you will, but I had something else in mind."

"Drenching him in whipped cream in the vein of *Carrie*?"

Zac chuckled. "Uh, no. Justin's a big boy. Would be an awful waste of whipped cream."

She sighed. "That's true. So what then?"

He draped her arms around his neck and pulled her to him. "You kiss me."

Sophie bit back a grin. "That's against the rules, you know. Dates are supposed to be purely for fun, purely platonic. No smexy stuff."

"I didn't say a thing about sex, but I like where your head is. In fact, let's work out the rest of that thought. Your place or mine?"

"You're such a flirt."

"Only with you." Then Zac turned her around and tucked her hair behind her ear. "Only with you."

"I love you," Sophie said, rising onto her toes to kiss him.

"I love you, too," Zac said. He pressed his lips to her neck, then the delicate skin below her ear and whispered, "Now about that smexy stuff . . ."

ABOUT THE AUTHOR

Melissa West writes heartfelt Southern romance and teen sci-fi romance, all with lots of kissing. Because who doesn't like kissing? She lives outside of Atlanta, Georgia, with her husband and two daughters and spends most of her time writing, reading, or fueling her coffee addiction.

For exclusive first looks at new projects, cover reveals, and fun giveaways, join Melissa's newsletter: http://www.melissawestauthor.com/newsletter.html

Racing Hearts

A Hamilton Stables Novel

MELISSA WEST

A Hamilton Stables
Novel

Silent
Hearts

MELISSA WEST

Wild Hearts

MELISSA WEST

www.ingramcontent.com/pod-product-compliance
Lightning Source LLC
Chambersburg PA
CBHW022154260626
47155CB00018B/1871